MITCH

JASPER SPRINGS

BOOK SIX

BY EVIE RILEY

Mitch

An MM Gay Awakening Romance

Jasper Springs

Book Six

MITCH

**A perpetual bachelor.
A sweet, tempting baker.
A chance to heal a wounded heart.**

Mitchell DeVille knows a piece of art when he sees it. After all, he's the hottest photographer in Jasper Springs. When Mitch discovers a fresh face at the wedding of the season, he can't turn away. And when his Pretty Boy muse offers him the chance to work together, he can't refuse.

Mitch soon discovers that the object of his desires is struggling with his newfound attraction, and he knows he shouldn't play with fire.

Penn Baker dreams of finding the perfect... someone. With a string of ex-girlfriends and one-night stands, he isn't sure there is anyone out there for a shy golden boy like him. Until he discovers a sexy, confident, photographer, that is.

As unusual feelings and desires rise in Penn, he finds himself falling fast for the charm of the man behind the camera.

Can Mitch be honest with himself about what he wants? Or will his high-built walls keep out more than just his fear of rejection?

Readers seeking a gay awakening romance set in a cozy little town may find this story checks those boxes. While Mitch and Penn may have cameos in other stories, each book in this series can be read as a standalone.

CHAPTER ONE

Mitch

"ALL RIGHT, JUST turn to your right a little more," I coaxed, practically holding my spine in the most unnatural position known to man. I arched myself like some sea serpent, back as far as I could go, just to get the one perfect shot.

Giselle's lips turned up into a perfect smile as she took my direction. A little more to my left, and the sun lit her up like an angel as her groom gazed upon her.

Click!

The fast clicks of the shutter echoed

in the air, capturing the moment in time, preserving it forever.

"Okay, I think I got what I need, thanks," I said as I forced my body back into an upright, natural position.

Aaron and Giselle scampered off hand in hand toward the doors of the Paradise Hotel, where everyone was gallivanting around on the terrace during cocktail hour.

I watched as the two of them ran off like two kids, snapping a few more candids as they did so.

But I couldn't deny my jealousy.

I loved my job, truly. Being a part of my clients' special occasions was something I didn't take lightly. I loved capturing the love between people, the stolen moments. Put simply, I loved love. I just wish it loved *me*.

My family couldn't understand how someone so entrenched in the business of love and weddings was a perpetual bachelor. It was a choice, I guess. Or at least that was what I told myself for years. It's a lot easier to run a self-employed business when you're the only one you have to answer to.

But lately, working weddings hadn't

felt the same.

I still loved photographing my clients but...

At the time, I had found myself feeling slighted by the over-presence of love in my life that had nothing to do with me.

I wanted those things, too, but it just didn't seem like it was going to happen. I'd been on dates, sure, but nothing ever really worked out. Not to mention the dating pool for an openly gay dude in Jasper Springs was practically nonexistent. When you lived in a small town like Jasper Springs, knowing everyone wasn't all it was cracked up to be. When you were the premier photographer for the county, and everyone knew your name and your business, it was even worse. Knowing everyone can have its advantages sure, but it made dating a fucking bitch.

I followed behind the happy couple, strolling up the expanse of the perfectly manicured green knoll, toward the marble steps of the Paradise's swanky terrace.

The guests were starting to arrive in full force, and so I made my rounds photographing candids of the guests and all the little details. The charcuterie boards, the champagne fountain, the gold foil etchings on the napkin.

Slipping past a group of black-tie suited guests, I made my way indoors to the Paradise's grand ballroom. The outside of the hotel was gorgeous, as architecturally it was practically something out of Gone With The Wind.

But inside?

It dripped opulence, with its sparkling chandeliers, white marble floors, and ornate, high vaulted ceilings.

I'd done a lot of weddings in Jasper Springs and the surrounding areas, but I had to admit, Giselle and Aaron's wedding took the cake. I was honestly surprised the fucking Pope didn't show up with the amount of people that turned out for their wedding.

Thankfully, both Giselle and Aaron's families were quite well off, so renting out the entirety of Jasper Springs's most sought after venue was nothing to them.

I sauntered around the inside, taking my detail photos, my candids of the arriving guests. Soon enough, it would be time for dinner, and I was fucking starving.

MITCH

My stomach grumbled, and I silently cursed myself. If I hadn't have been so rushed that morning because I overslept, I would have had time to eat more than a pop tart and a mocha Double Shot.

The breakfast of photographers everywhere.

I found my way over to the elaborately decorated wedding cake, which was all of five tiers. Though, I guess it fit right in with Giselle's style, the layers of ivory cream speckled with gold leaf and deep, burgundy flowers cascading down the side.

I set up my camera, working the angles of the giant cake, noting the smoothness of the icing. I'd seen a lot of cakes in my years, but this one was absolutely perfect. It almost didn't look real.

A part of me was impressed, knowing the disasters that could happen when transporting a cake, especially one that big.

After taking my shots, I turned to do some crowd photos, noticing as I scanned the room, someone I most certainly didn't recognize.

He was dressed far more casual than

the rest of the guests, which told me he was likely hired help.

Perhaps he was with the catering or the Paradise event staff?

I settled my lens as I looked through, noticing his side profile. With the zoom on and the lens I was using, the chandeliers and background blurred into bokeh—a soft, out-of-focus background with faded glittery spots—as Pretty Boy and his side profile became the focus.

From the angle, his blond hair caught flecks of gold from the chandeliers, his pale blue eyes standing out in stark contrast against his fair complexion and dark lashes.

He casually cocked his head in thought, his wistful gaze set on someone or something, but that didn't matter to me.

Snap!

I watched through my lens as he licked his lips, as his eyebrows furrowed, and something in my chest snapped at the same time as the shutter.

I understood that look of longing.

That look of wishful thinking.

I lowered my camera, if only for a moment, gazing at Pretty Boy in his lavender button down, looking at a couple dancing. The look of heartbreak on his face was unmistakable, and I had the craziest feeling, that I wanted to go over there and *hug* him. Maybe even ask him to dance, if only to take his mind off something that was causing him such evident pain. Despite the fact I didn't know how to dance like half the people were on the dance floor to whatever cocktail hour shit was being played.

Surely such a thing was crazy, right?

I didn't even know the guy.

"Mitch! There you are!" Grayson said, his bright Colgate-smile tearing me away from the nameless Pretty Boy.

I gazed up at the bride's brother, dressed to the nines, of course, in his flashy tux, with a martini in hand.

"Something I can do for you, Grayson?" I asked, glancing back to see mystery pretty boy had disappeared.

"Actually, there is," he said, flashing me a grin.

CHAPTER TWO

Penn

I THOUGHT BEING back in Jasper Springs would be a good thing, but as I looked around the Paradise, I wondered if perhaps I'd been out of the Jasper Springs loop for far too long.

Four years *was* a long time when you came from a small town like Jasper Springs.

Where everyone knew everyone, and everything was always picture perfect.

Take the bride of this wedding, for example, Giselle.

Her family was one of the most well

known in Jasper Springs, and her husband also came from another well known, wealthy family in the area. Their families were involved in everything, just like the Rhodes, and loved by nearly *all* of Jasper Springs for their philanthropy, their parties and soirees.

Even Giselle's brother, Grayson—who was the talk of the town years ago for his *scandalous* tryst with his sister's ex, of all things—seemed to have the *perfect* life with his new boyfriend.

I wished I could have that.

The ease of self, the happy ever after.

I thought the change of scenery was what I needed, when I left for pastry school, but sadly, my life was not a Jasper Springs success story.

Aside from a few one night stands that ended awkwardly with the girls leaving me to stew in mortification, a couple girlfriends, and my too close parents constantly trying to play matchmaker, I'd practically given up on dating.

Maybe I was just meant to be alone.

So, instead of going out and meeting people like my mother suggested, like a normal twenty-three year old, I turned to the one thing I knew I could do well.

Bake.

My parents had owned Penn's Bakery—affectionately named after their only child, me—since I was in middle school. While they weren't the only bakery in Jasper Springs, they were pretty well known in the county. My mother's macaroons are *to die for.* I swore she could compete on Great British Bake Off with those things.

Who cares if she hasn't been home to London in twenty years.

No, as usual, instead of socializing like a normal twenty-three year old, I locked myself in my parent's bakery—my birthright as my father would say—and took out my perpetual singledom and emo woes on the giant five tier spectacle Giselle had ordered for her wedding. I got lost in the flowers, brushing and smoothing the buttercream on each individual tier. Every little detail was a welcome relief as I strategically placed each flower and accent.

I'd always loved weddings, and had fond memories of my mom baking for weddings and parties growing up. Our small house was overtaken by mom's cake and cookie orders, since in those early days before they opened the shop she'd work from home.

And when I'd ultimately ended up at home on a Friday night, because I was the awkward kid who didn't fit in anywhere, she'd always let me help.

Though now, I was doing more than helping. Now that I had my certifications, my degree, I could finally take on more responsibility with the shop.

My dad wouldn't admit it, and I knew my mom would say otherwise, but I was no fool. I knew that they were looking at retirement, just *waiting* for the right moment. Waiting for me to graduate, move home, and take over the family business. I knew what my future looked like.

But I also knew I wanted to love more than just my job.

I wanted to share my life with someone the way my mom and dad did.

But no matter how many women they set me up with, or how many times someone swiped right on me...

Nothing ever felt right.

And then I came to the Paradise, on a

job, and I saw *him.*

Over in the corner by my masterpiece.

He was tall, dark, and handsome like the men in the fairytales always were. A little rogue-ish looking, which told me he was definitely *not* a guest. The wedding was a black-tie affair, but my mom assured me my button down and slacks would be enough. After all, I came home a week earlier, due to a glitch in the computer system regarding my train ticket, so it wasn't like I was planning on going to a fancy wedding.

Not to mention the closest suit shop was in the city, and I *hated* going into the city. All those people, the traffic...

Mr. Tall, Dark, and Handsome leaned against the table, looking like he was bored to tears.

I swallowed harshly, feeling strangely hot, like I was going to get caught with my hand in the cookie jar or something.

Which was an odd way to feel about some stranger, some man who looked like something right out of a romance novel or something.

A part of me felt compelled by his apathetic expression, the way he *sexily* leaned against the table like he was the King of the castle or something.

But I was frozen in place, scared to move, to even *breathe* in his vicinity.

What the hell?

My cock twitched in my pants, and a maddening blush crept up my cheeks.

Now was certainly not an appropriate time for an erection!

My brain was a bit slow to process, and that's when I felt more embarrassed than ever. Not because of where I was, but because...

What the fuck?

I'd never been attracted to men before, like *at all.*

I thought surely, something must be off, maybe I got a whiff of some perfume, or maybe I, too, was suffering from boredom.

Or maybe it's because I haven't jacked off since I came home.

I shoved the weird and inappropriate thoughts out of my mind though, because my *mother,* of all people, broke my concentration.

"Penn, sweetheart, I've been looking everywhere for you."

"Huh?" I shook my head, dispelling

the strange moment. I turned back to look in the direction of the hot stranger, noticing he was gone. Maybe I'd imagined it. Maybe he was some sort of sex-deprived mirage.

Could dry spells cause hallucinations?

I wasn't sure.

"Our work here is done," she said, taking in the sea of people as the bride and groom made their way around the tables to socialize.

I scanned the crowd once more for my mirage, but he truly was nowhere to be seen.

That's it, I'm definitely losing my marbles.

"Penn..." she said, snapping her fingers, pulling my attention back to her once more.

"Okay," I said, swatting at her hand, her perfectly manicured nails smacking my palm.

"We're heading out, come on," she said, looping her arm in my mine, leading me out of the Paradise Hotel.

CHAPTER THREE

Penn

IT SHOULD HAVE been a downright shame that I was at home, in my boxers and under my blue flannel comforter before nine thirty.

My parents were usually in bed by eight, what with keeping baker's hours my entire life.

Aside from a few times my classmates and I went out, I was mostly the same.

There was a simplicity to my routine, but that night I couldn't get comfortable, despite feeling practically exhausted from a long work day.

The house was quiet, and I knew I was the only one awake, which didn't help matters.

My mind was strangely alert, but then again, doomscrolling social media probably wasn't helping matters.

I wasn't the jealous type by any means, but if I had a nickel for every post I saw of a classmate getting married or having kids, I swore I could open my own bakery.

I'd never really thought about getting married or having kids in the sense that I imagined myself with my exes making cheesy and annoying posts like that.

I'd always known I would get married and have kids someday, much like a kid knows Christmas is coming. You don't question it, but the day itself varies and the gifts aren't always the same.

When I thought about what I wanted in my future, that's what came to mind, but I hadn't met anyone I could envision my cookie cutter Hallmark Happy Ending with just yet.

I continued to scroll as I thought about the wedding.

About all the couples dancing, the bride and groom smiling ear to ear.

MITCH

The hot stranger standing by my cake.

Instantly, my cock twitched in my boxers, reminding me of my embarrassment from earlier. Except, there was nothing to be embarrassed about in the privacy of my own bedroom.

Maybe I really did just need to bust out a good nut.

Nonchalantly, I slid my hand in between my boxers, gently pulling and brushing my thumb over my head as I set my phone down with my free hand.

I eased into my pillows, beneath my covers, building a slow rhythm. I closed my eyes, clearing my mind to focus on the feel of my hand, the thrust as I tightened my grip.

Steadily, I increased my pace, my palm already wet from the precum soaking my head. It was warm, sticky, and for some reason, it turned me on a lot more than it usually did.

I gripped my shaft, squeezing as my breath hitched. I stopped only for a moment, to spit in my hand, to get myself *real* wet and slippery. I slid my boxers off, needing the freedom of movement. Underneath the covers, I throbbed with need. I grabbed myself once more, lathering my cock in my spit.

The touch of my hand against my rock hard cock, my thumb brushing over my rigid veins felt *so good.*

And then the strangest thought popped into my brain.

A hot, wet tongue licking my shaft, from my balls to my head, taking me into the back of his throat, while he cupped my balls, squeezing them until I—

Before I could even process such an anomaly of thought, I came.

"Oh fuck..." I cursed under my breath, scrambling to cover the spewing geyser that was my cock, if only because I didn't want dried jizz on the inside of my comforter.

My body shook as my cock pulsed, coating my hand, and my entire body practically melted into the mattress.

"Everyone has an off day, Penn, that's all it is," I told myself, swallowing harshly as the thought dissipated in my brain.

"It doesn't mean anything," I said, reaching in my drawer for a towel with my free, clean hand.

I took my time cleaning up, trying to focus on *anything* but the weird image my mind had formed to get me off.

What was my deal today?

First that hot stranger, now this?

Maybe my lack of a sex life really was affecting my mental state. I should probably look into that.

Pulling my underwear back on, I settled into bed once more, but a harsh object poked me in the back.

"Ow!" I yelped as I reached behind me, pulling out my phone.

Of course, how could I have forgotten.

Just as I went to plug it in, I noticed I'd been tagged. Or more or less, the bakery had been tagged. The bakery's Facebook page saw more action than my personal one, which was just another reason I'd given up on socializing.

I scrolled through the images of the wedding, coming across some beautiful images of the cake. Truly, I'd never seen images like them before. The angles, the detail. I wondered if I could use said pictures for my cake portfolio.

I clicked my way around until I found the name of the photographer.

De*Vil Photography was the name of the company. Clicking on the page, I noted their tagline was *the devil's in the* *details,* pasted across a collage of artfully done black and white images that captured people in various states. Silhouettes of brides, little kid hands inside of their parents holding flowers, even an image of two men embracing on Main Street under the streetlights, the light refracting off the puddles of rain.

I squinted as I tried to make out their dark features. One of them looked like that Rhodes guy, the one who was always in the paper. Weston or Westley or something or other.

Scrolling down the page, I looked for their information, fully intent on emailing them to ask if I could use their photos, when an idea popped into my head.

As I clicked through their portfolio, it was apparent that they were really good at what they did, not just by the photos they'd posted of the wedding tonight already, but in every wedding album, the photographs of the cakes, the cookies.

I knew mom and dad had no clue when it came to social media, or digital content.

I'd started an Instagram in college for the bakery as a side project, but until recently I hadn't focused on it at all, being as I wasn't home.

I'd showed my mom numerous times how to take a picture with her phone and upload it, but clearly she wasn't as invested in the technological advances of business nowadays.

But that was my job, wasn't it?

To take over the operations?

To bring Penn's bakery into the twenty-first century?

Which was why I didn't think twice about messaging Mr. De*Vil about the use of his photos of my masterpiece, as well as potentially collaborating on a social media campaign for the bakery.

I figured it couldn't hurt to reach out, right?

CHAPTER FOUR

Mitch

I SAT BACK in my editing chair, watching as the loading page did its thing, taking forever for my post to actually post.

While it would take me a while to really cull through and edit the wedding of the century, I needed to at least post a couple candids or favorites to keep both my clients and my followers clicking.

After getting home so early, I had more than enough time to hand edit a few shots of the details to keep everyone satisfied while I worked on the main attraction, the bride and groom.

So, I'd opted to showcase the Paradise in all its matrimonial glory, from the sparkling chandelier to the spectacular cake, the overflowing charcuterie board and towers of champagne.

Finally, the post went through.

I looked at the clock on my computer, which read nine thirty. I debated if I should keep going as I swiveled back and forth in my chair.

Staying up late editing photos wasn't my favorite way to spend a Saturday night, but it wasn't like I had anything else going on.

Which was pretty pathetic, if you asked me.

God is this like the pre-thirty jitters or something?

What the fuck is wrong with me?

Just as I moved to close out my browser, I saw the familiar little red notification letting me know I had a message.

I groaned, wondering for a moment if I should ignore the message and get back to whoever it was in the morning, but I couldn't help myself, and checked it out.

When I saw the photograph in the icon, next to the name Penn Baker, I sat up straighter. I clicked the photo, viewing his profile instantly.

Despite it being set to private, I could see enough photographs to confirm my sudden shock.

Pretty Boy had a name, and apparently the star Baker was a... baker?

How on point can you get when your last name is your profession?

Then again, I had no room to talk because my family literally owned *M's Place*, the local watering hole, and had named the bar after all three of us. My brother Miguel, myself, and my younger sister, Max, and not to mention, my photography business was a play on my last name, DeVille.

I couldn't help myself as I scrolled through the available information, which showed Pretty Boy's most recent profile picture of him standing outside Penn's Bakery on Charleston Street.

I'd been to the place a dozen times, mostly when I needed to grab something to bring to a potluck or a holiday gathering, but still.

The photograph showed him dressed in blue jeans and red and white converse that matched his red and white striped shirt. A bright, wide smile that reached his eyes gazed back at me, his toasted marshmallow colored hair blowing in the breeze like he was doing a photoshoot for the Disney Channel or something.

God, he was fucking *adorable*.

I smirked as I came back to my inbox, glancing over his message, the light of the computer bathing me in artificial anonymity.

I read over his message, asking about using the images of the cake for the bakery's social media page, followed by an *inquiry* about working together. It wouldn't be the first time someone asked to partner up with me for my services, but it was definitely the first time I wanted to say *yes,* without even a second thought.

Even if it's only because the little cinnamon roll looks positively delicious.

I typed back with a smirk on my face.

All right, Penn, I'll bite. I could use a little sugar in my portfolio. Let's meet up and discuss our... partnership over coffee.

MITCH

Say tomorrow afternoon, if you're free?

I hit send, leaning back in my chair, grinning like a little kid.

Was it unprofessional of me to flirt with a potential client?

Probably.

But the perks of working for myself was I could do whatever the fuck I wanted to do. I was the HR department, baby.

Penn responded rather quickly, which only fueled my confidence more.

What's your favorite sugary snack? I can bring something if you like.

Oh, he made this too easy.

Sweet little cinnamon rolls who message me at nine thirty at night.

Maybe I had no shame, but a part of me didn't really care what people thought of me. Either Penn would find my personality fun and easy, or he would get his little tighty whities up in a twist and turn the other way, which was possible.

But honestly, if he was *that* uptight with his masculinity that he couldn't take some light flirting or teasing, I didn't want to work with a stick in the mud.

To my chagrin, he responded with, *I'm more of a cream puff, actually.*

A dark chuckle escaped my throat.

Alrighty then, game on, Penn Baker.

Fluffy, delicious, and full of sweet cream. Just the way I like.

For a moment, even I thought I'd gone too far. Light teasing and flirting was one thing, but the squirrel in my brain who was my HR department flashed a very large *WARNING!* in my brain.

Thankfully, Penn's response didn't call me a fucking perv.

Instead, it was the opposite.

What time should we meet up?

I chuckled, noting how he hadn't responded to my obvious overstep, but the fact he still wanted to meet up, even after my faux pas told me he was interested perhaps in more than just photographs.

Pretty Boy wants to play hard to get, that's fine.

How does twelve thirty sound, Cream Puff? I messaged.

Penn responded quickly.

Sounds good to me, Cupcake.

I let out an actual laugh at his words

MITCH

as I messaged him back, telling him I'd
see his sweet ass tomorrow afternoon.

CHAPTER FIVE

Mitch

THE CAFE WAS always bustling at lunchtime, but honestly, I preferred the crowd. It provided me with a multitude of entertainment. I always noticed the little things no one else did. The barista behind the counter who couldn't stop staring at the dishwasher's ass, the teacher running late to his class because he was deep in doomscrolling TikTok, the feuding couple in the corner who were practically vibrating with sexual tension as they drank their coffees in silence.

I leaned back in my chair, my gaze sweeping over the room, watching to see what small town excitement was afoot today, when the door jingled. I turned to see Penn, carrying a pink box, dressed like he was going to the fucking Science Fair. He wore pale khakis and a deep blue button down with pale blue dots all over it, his golden-brown hair swept to the side like Justin Bieber in his *Baby Baby* era.

Which should have been off-putting, but for some reason it wasn't.

My cock twitched as my stomach growled.

Delectable, indeed.

"Well, I'll be damned, if those are really cream puffs in there, I might kiss you," I teased as he took a seat, setting down the package.

I didn't miss the blush spreading across his fair cheeks, and my cock twitched again, my mind immediately thinking about other parts of Pretty Boy's body that would look *so nice* with a little pink tint.

"Well, a deal is a deal, right?" he said, tucking some stray hair behind his ear as he pushed the box toward me.

MITCH

I smirked as I pushed the lid open, my eyes widening when I saw about a dozen cream puffs stuffed to the brim, their thick pastry cream seeping out of their tiny holes. The scent of vanilla cream and strawberries made my stomach growl again, and my mouth was practically salivating as I took in the sight of the cupcake in the center. The icing was whipped, sprinkled with bits of strawberries and red syrupy sauce that dripped down the sides. Even though it was in a cardboard box, the presentation was still gorgeous.

I glanced up at Penn, who was watching me intently. I pulled out a cream puff, plopping it into my mouth, if only to quiet my stomach and my damn erection.

It was fucking amazing.

"Mmmmm." I groaned as the sweetness of the pastry cream hit my tongue.

"Glad to see I can please your sweet tooth," he said with a shy smile.

I went for another cream puff, because sue me, they were delicious.

"Too bad I left my camera at home. Your little tableau is quite creative."

I watched as his smile spread wide from the praise, and that didn't help the matter of my unruly erection one bit.

It would appear my little Cream Puff likes praise. Well noted.

"Oh, I, uh, the cupcake was a last minute thing. I wasn't sure if you were a vanilla guy, or—"

"Oh, I assure you, Penn, I am not vanilla in any shape of the word," I said with a smirk, wiping some stray cream off of my lips.

I watched with interest as Penn's entire face turned a shade of red I'd only ever seen on fire hydrants, and he physically *squirmed* in his seat.

He cleared his throat, and I couldn't help but grin.

Oh, this is going to be fun.

"Penn? Penn Baker, is that you?" a saccharine voice disturbed our bubble.

I watched as the color drained from Penn's face and his eyes widened in fear.

"A... Amy... Hi..." he said as he crossed his legs, his entire body *tensing* at the sight of her. He looked up at her, swallowing harshly.

She was average height with short blonde hair, a round face, and deep brown eyes. She was also dressed in a tight, low-cut red dress and black boots, and looked like she could pass as Penn's Disney Channel co-star.

She looked familiar, but I couldn't place her. Then again, in my line of work, sometimes people just blended together.

Amy tucked her hair behind her ear as she coyly made eyes at my Cream Puff, and a spark of jealousy fired inside of me.

Which was irrational, right?

I barely even *knew* the guy...

"Amy, this is..."

"Mitchell DeVille. I know who you are," she said with a giggle.

I leaned back casually in my seat, catching her gaze.

"And you would be..." I drawled.

"Penn and I dated for a semester in college."

I looked from her to him, watching as he chewed his lip.

Oh.

Oh... shit.

Was I wrong?

Was Pretty Boy not who I thought he was?

At that exact moment as I questioned my gaydar, I saw him steal a glance at me.

And it was enough for me to understand, that this... This was uncharted territory for my little Cream Puff.

That should have been enough to deter me. I'd been in the game long enough, and I was open about my sexuality.

But Penn clearly was not.

Though I wasn't sure if it was just a case of being in the closet, or if I genuinely had a bi or gay awakening on my hands.

I knew I should have walked away then. Said thanks for the cream puffs and called it a day, and given him a license to use the photos from the wedding for his promotional needs.

But I liked a *challenge*. Both in my work, and in my personal life.

I smiled, nodding at Penn, if only to try and quell his panic.

Don't worry, baby, I won't spill your secrets.

"Penn and I are colleagues, isn't that right, Penn?" I said, giving him the floor, the chance to control the narrative.

I knew firsthand how important that was when you were trying to figure it all out. When you didn't have the answers yet.

Penn's shoulders loosened as he looked at me with a soft smile, and I knew.

The man was going to ruin me.

But maybe I like a little destruction.

"Yeah, colleagues. Mitch is, uh, doing some work for me. For the bakery."

Amy teetered back and forth as she looked between us.

"Oh, of course, duh! Mitchell is like *the best* photographer. I'm sure whatever he's doing for you, will be so worth it."

Penn smiled, but it wasn't genuine. Beneath the sparkle in his eyes, I could still see the panic.

"Totally," he said, running his hand through his hair.

"I thought you were still up north," she said.

Penn shook his head, tapping his fingers on the table. His gaze fixed on her face, never once venturing below to her prominent cleavage or the way she twirled her hair.

Watching her flirt with him made me angry, jealous, even though I knew that was insane.

I watched intently as he settled his hands in his lap.

"I was… but I graduated, so I'm home now."

"Oh that's awesome! Congratulations!" she said as she clasped her hands together in front of her bountiful cleavage.

I raised my eyebrow in disgust.

Oh honey, you are barking up the wrong tree, clearly.

"Thanks," he said sheepishly.

"I hate to interrupt this little High School Reunion, but we are kind of in the middle of a meeting, *Amy*," I said.

The tone of command and possession in my voice was not missed, even to me.

Penn eased in his seat as Amy focused on me instead.

"Oh, I'm so sorry! I didn't mean to be rude, I just wanted to say *hey!*" she said, waving. "I'll leave you two to talk business, but Penn…" She sighed, chewing her lip.

"Hmmm?" he asked, looking up, his expression pained.

"We should hang out sometime."

Yeah, I bet her idea of hanging out is Netflix and Chill. Sans the Netflix.

Penn nodded. "Mhmm. Totally," he said hurriedly.

I watched as she teetered off out the door, turning my attention back to Penn.

"She's... cute," I said, deadpan.

Penn slid down in his chair, running his hand through his golden locks.

"I mean, I guess," he said softly.

"Seems like a nice girl."

Penn sighed, his voice full of disappointment. "She is."

"But?" I asked calmly.

"I mean, you know how it is... I just didn't see us going anywhere," he murmured.

I bet you didn't, Cream Puff.

I popped another cream puff into my mouth.

"And where is it *you* want to go, Penn?" I asked.

I was only busting his balls, to try and lighten the mood, but a part of me wanted to know the answer.

What *did* Penn Baker want, really?

Penn sighed, sitting up straighter.

"It doesn't matter. You're a busy guy,

and so am I, so I won't take up too much more of your time with my personal drama," he said, his shoulders falling as he pursed his lips.

"Ah, yes... this is the part where you sell your soul to me," I said, flashing him with a smirk.

I watched as the corner of Penn's mouth started to rise, the hint of a smile fighting its way out from the frown on his adorable, sweet face.

"One week in general should be sufficient, I think. You can come to the bakery, see how we operate, take some candids as well as still life shots."

I raised my brow. "Still life, huh? You minor in art *up north*?" I asked.

Penn shook his head.

"No. Pastry, but... my dad paints in his spare time."

"Usually, I charge by the hour, but—"

"I'll pay you whatever it is you want," he blurted out, and I couldn't help but smile at his desperation.

He was so cute, I couldn't stand it. I just wanted him to ease up, to feel better.

"I was going to say... but, for you, I can do a flat rate of six hundred for the week, and this next part is the most important part of the negotiation," I said, leaning closer.

Penn leaned in without hesitation, putting his face inches away from mine. He smelled like sugar, spice, and untapped desire.

I gently pulled the box of goodies toward me as I whispered, "I'm going to need another box of cream puffs, and maybe a sweet, spicy, cinnamon roll. As terms of the payment, of course," I said, flashing him a grin.

Penn's gaze fell to my lips, and I watched him swallow harshly, his Adam's apple bobbing as a soft *sigh* escaped him.

This is a bad idea.

Penn looked up at me with glassy, turquoise eyes, biting his bottom lip, and my cock twitched once more from the sight.

"Deal," he said.

My gaze dropped to his lips. Pink, pouty, and perfect.

Fuck.

If he had been any other man, I would've just gone for it. I would've closed the gap and kissed him, but somehow I knew I needed to take my time with Penn.

I knew kissing him like this, now, would only push him away. So, for the moment, I stowed my desire, my sudden attraction, in favor of being *professional* and giving my Cream Puff the space he needed to process everything that had just happened.

"I'll start Monday," I said, pulling back.

CHAPTER SIX

Mitch

"WHAT'S WITH THE face?" Dawson asked, poking me in the side like a juvenile.

I took a sip of my beer as Weston flirted relentlessly with his boyfriend, my oldest friend, Cade.

Dawson and Cade were probably the closest thing I had to what one would call a *best friend*. Cade and I had hung out since middle school, and after he and Dawson broke up, the guy refused to leave. But with that being said, I actually enjoyed his idiocy most of the time.

When I was in a better mood that was.

"What face?" I deadpanned as Nolan came back to the table with a handful of drinks. True to his white knight nature, Cade immediately moved to help him, abandoning whatever Weston was going on about.

"Thanks," Nolan said, his glasses sliding down his nose in the process as the liquid sloshed around in the glasses. Miraculously, nothing spilled as Cade helped pass out drinks.

"The constipated face you're currently making," Dawson nipped. "I would think you'd still be smiling from ear to ear from the wedding. I know I am," he said, grinning like the Cheshire Cat for added idiot effect.

Dawson was like that.

Like a big, dumb golden retriever. Most of the time, I didn't mind.

But Dawson was right, I was in a mood, and I had been ever since Amy showed up to crash my date—no, *meeting*—with Penn.

It wasn't like I thought Cream Puff and I were going to run off into the sunset after one box of baked goods and some stupid flirting, so why did it bother me so much?

"Yeah, well, you don't have over three thousand images to cull for editing either," I snapped back.

Weston took a sip of his drink before wrapping his arm around Cade *again,* for like the fifth time since they'd arrived only an hour ago, which was also irritating me.

Fuck, maybe I just need to get shitfaced to forget about this weird ass day... Go home and work on some photos.

"No, that's not it," Weston mulled, his tone accusatory.

I shot him a glare.

Since he'd started dating Cade, he made it his business to know *everything* about our little group.

Who was crushing on who, what social gala was I photographing next, was everyone free for Poker on Sunday?

It was nice to have someone in the group to take over organizing shit, but it also got on my nerves.

Aside from my jobs, I didn't schedule shit. I liked the spontaneity of life and *not* knowing what was going to happen or where I was going to end up.

I looked at my friends, canoodling with their boyfriends like some gay version of the Stepford Wives, and it only pissed me off even more.

"Weston's right, something else is on your mind. I can tell." Dawson poked me in the ribs again, and I smacked his hand.

"Come on, Mitch, let it out. I promise you'll feel better," Dawson teased.

Nolan rolled his eyes. "If he doesn't want to talk about it, leave the guy alone."

I shot an appreciative glance at Nolan, the newest addition to the group. A part of me had to give the guy props, for being Dawson's other half couldn't have been easy.

And from what I'd seen, Nolan might be the only person on the planet who could actually get Dawson to *stop* and sit still, to be quiet, with just a damn *look*.

Knowing Dawson, it was probably some sort of sex role-play thing, but I liked to think underneath all of that steam, it was more than that.

I saw the way he *looked* at the pencil pusher.

I'd give my left nut for some pretty boy to look at me like that.

Pretty Boy...

I sighed, figuring fighting the truth was moot.

Besides, I was on my second beer of the night, and I hadn't even gotten to karaoke yet.

"Nothing. I just have, like, the worst gaydar on the planet sometimes."

A resounding, "Oh," followed from Dawson, louder than it should have been.

"Rejected by a straight man?" Weston nonchalantly drawled.

"Worse," I admitted as Nolan pushed Dawson in the chest, the two of them play-fighting over something.

"Worse?" Cade asked, his eyebrows furrowing as his baby blues fixated their concerned gaze on me.

"I think I have a fucking awakening on my hands."

Nolan let out a, "Fuck," while Weston only shrugged.

"I don't see the problem," Weston said as I took another sip of my own drink.

"Yeah, well, you may be the type to just roll in and command shit, Wes, but some of us actually have to play by the rules. Especially when it involves our jobs," I snarled.

"So, you're working with him?" Nolan pressed.

I sighed, figuring there was no use denying it.

"Sort of. We met today to go over the job. Some social media campaign stuff, and..."

"And what?" Dawson pressed as I scanned the room.

At that moment, just as I opened my mouth, I saw him. He'd just walked in, alone, with another one of those pink boxes, looking like a lost kitten.

My heart lurched in my chest as I swatted at Dawson, excusing myself from the table.

"Fine, it's my turn to sing anyway," Dawson touted from behind me, but his voice was white noise.

CHAPTER SEVEN

Penn

"ALL RIGHT, MIGUEL said he has his sister corralled in the stock room, so we have, like, ten minutes tops to get this shit set up," Archie, my best friend slash co-worker, said as we entered the bar.

The DeVille siblings who owned and worked at the bar were notorious for their over the top birthday battle. According to my mom, they'd been one-upping each other for a decade now. But I never paid attention to stuff like that.

I was always just focused on studying, or baking. I was never the kid who went out and socialized, even when I did live here.

I had to admit though, as an only child a part of me was always envious when I heard stories about siblings having fun at one another's expense.

It was a small window to get set up, but it was a window still, so instead of dreaming about siblings I'd never have, I focused on the task at hand.

Archie and I could work pretty fast. We'd set up much more elaborate tables than a cake and cupcake bar on the fly.

Will, the DJ, saw us and immediately came over to help Archie and I with our boxes while some patron wailed out to Nickelback on stage.

Seriously, dude should not quit his day job.

"I know, I know," I said as I gingerly pulled out the cake, setting it on a high top in the corner by the Love-Meter machine.

That's when I saw him. Across the room, sitting with a group of guys, who were all over one another.

A blush crept up my cheeks.

M's Place was well known for it's queer-friendly atmosphere, but I couldn't say I spent a lot of time there. Not because knowing that freaked me out, I just...

Somewhere in my DNA, I missed the link that made me able to engage in situations like this.

I wanted to go out and party, and karaoke... but I was always working, or studying. The few times I *did* go out, only ended with one night stands where the girls ran out the morning after anyway, so I didn't have the best track record or experience with bar culture.

Hell, who was I kidding, I didn't have the best experience with *people*, period.

I was better off frosting cakes for people who actually *knew* how to have fun.

But something about Mitchell DeVille called to the little voice inside of me, begging me to let go.

To have *fun*.

I swallowed as I watched his friends smiling, kissing one another, and being unabashedly public about their affections.

Then reality hit me like a sack of flour as I put two and two together.

His flirting online and at the cafe, his

very PDA friendly friends, the way he was currently looking at me... like he wanted to *devour* me whole...

Oh fuck...

"What's got you all in a twist? Hot young thing? Ex-girlfriend? Hot ex-girlfriend with another hot ex-girlfriend?" Archie snarked as he set down the boxes of cookies and cupcakes, popping the lids.

"Nothing. I—"

But it was no use; Archie's radar was laser sharp. He'd laid eyes on Mitchell, who was now getting up from his seat, and walking toward the bar.

"Oh... so... hot guy then. Hmmm," he said with a shrug as my entire body heated from his words.

"Archie!"

"That is not nothing," Archie jabbed.

"Oh my God, Archie, it's not like that. He's a—"

What could I say?

Friend didn't seem like the right word, but we weren't strangers either, right?

"He's a... work... friend."

Archie raised his eyebrows. "Mhmmm. Sure. I have to say I'm kind of surprised, though," he said, shaking his head as I fought to refute his insinuations.

"Didn't think guys did it for you," he teased.

"They don't... I mean—"

How could I explain something I barely understood myself?

I was not sure *anyone* really did it for me. It wasn't like I had a ton of experience with people in general. I'd dated a few girls, and while I didn't *mind* fucking, especially from behind, I would have rather ingested a year old cake than go down on a girl.

Does that mean I'm gay?

"You're blushing like a whore in church, Penn. Besides, that man has more flames than a bag of Hot Cheetos. You can't hide that shit."

My stomach twisted in knots as I tried *not* to look at the tall, dark, cocky photographer.

And damn, was it a fight not to look.

"He's right you know," Will said as the last notes of the song played out. "You're about as subtle as a hurricane."

"He's coming over here," Archie said giddily. "Be cool, be cool... You gotta make a man work for it, baby."

Mortification spread across my cheeks, through my veins, and caused my stomach to flip.

"What? No, Archie, I swear... I—"

Archie smirked as I tried to find some sort of escape route, but between the tables with Max's goodies, the bar, and the crowd, I was stuck.

"I can't do this right now, I have to—" Panic crept up my neck with the maddening heat of a blush I couldn't seem to quiet if my life depended on it.

Will laughed as he turned away from us, calling out over his microphone that he needed the patrons' *assistance* to wish Max a happy birthday.

"Miguel said five minutes, Penn," Archie whispered, just as Mitchell made it to the bar.

I felt him before I saw him, as I tried to focus and busy myself with arranging the cupcakes around the cake.

"Hey," he said nonchalantly, leaning on the edge of the bar.

"Hey..." I said, like an absolute idiot as I turned around to get a look at him. Under the pink and blue lights of the bar, Mitchell looked stunning. Like some actor on an HBO show or something.

My cock more than agreed with the assessment, which made me acutely aware that whatever was happening to me, I was in over my head.

Never in my life had I looked at any woman, even the ones I'd dated, and formed an *instant* boner.

Panic flooded me as I shifted my body toward the table, if only to hide my inappropriate erection.

What the fuck?

Under his steely neon gaze, I felt like I couldn't breathe. I couldn't process all the stimuli assaulting me at once.

"What brings you to this hole in the wall?" he asked, shifting his stance as he focused his gaze on me.

I felt like I was going to spontaneously combust.

I swallowed harshly as I turned away from him, needing air.

Why was *talking* to him so difficult?

I talked to lots of people!

"I mean... it's your sister's birthday."

Mitchell raised one eyebrow. "So?"

I motioned to the cake. "Birthdays are kind of my job."

"That sounds horrible," he said with a

grin.

"It's not so bad... sometimes, I guess," I said, running a hand through my hair, if only because I was feeling more on the spot than if I'd have had to karaoke in front of this entire damn room.

"I can't say I'm surprised. This has Miguel written all over it," Mitchell said, nodding to the cake. "Does that say... Happy Birthday *Bitch*?"

I blushed at his curse. Something about the way his voice sounded when he swore made my damn blood rush and my cock twitch.

Please, just kill me now.

"It was requested," I replied, but because I was nervous, I started rambling.

So unprofessional.

"I made a cake that said Merry Fucking Christmas once. My classmate and I piped on some bare assed elves. It was a hit at his Christmas party."

Why the fuck did I say that?

Mitchell smirked, his eyes alight with mischief.

"What's the dirtiest cake you've made, Cream Puff?"

My cheeks heated from his cocky

tone, and before I could answer, thankfully, I was saved by the bell.

Or rather, Archie strong-arming his way to light the candles on the cake.

"S'cuse me," he said, knocking me into Mitchell. Because of the tight space, I nearly fell over, but Mitchell caught me by the arms.

I was acutely aware of his warm palms against my skin, making the rest of my body heat like an oven. Instinctively, I reached out to steady myself, my hands settling on his hips as I cursed from the shove, both mortified beyond all belief, and the slightest bit pissed that Archie would be so careless.

Someone could have gotten seriously hurt!

"What the Hell, Archie?" I growled as I removed my sweaty hands from Mitchell's hips, fidgeting with my shirt and pants, if only to quell the burgeoning hardness that would not relent.

The last thing I needed was Mitchell noticing such things.

A strange sort of thought presented itself as I had to acknowledge a part of me that wondered what his reaction would be if...

I forced the thought down, moving away from Mitchell for the moment as Will called out for everyone to sing Happy Birthday.

My focus was pulled to the end of the bar, as Miguel forced Max along the hallway out into the open bar area.

The shock on her face was evident, and I could see she was cursing him up and down, but despite that, there was a light in her eyes that could not be mistaken when she set gaze on her cake.

A two-tiered cake trimmed in white and pink fondant, with small liquor bottles and fondant bulldog faces.

I didn't understand the reference, but then again, I didn't need to. Whatever language they had as siblings was understood, and that was all that mattered.

The look of happiness on her face made me smile, too. It settled all my nerves, and made me feel a thousand times better, because that one look...

That look of sheer delight was why I loved baking.

Bringing joy to the little moments in life, not just the big ones, was what I loved most about baking and designing.

The sounds of off-key and off-timed renditions of Happy Birthday filled the air, and I couldn't help but join in as I moved aside, making room for Max and Miguel.

Max stood in front of her cake, and as the last notes of the out of sync bar hummed her birthday serenade, she took a moment to pause.

To make a wish.

I wondered for a moment what she wished for, and then watched as she blew out each flame one by one.

Watched as one candle flickered back to life as the bar roared with laughter and "oohs" and "awwws" filled the space.

"Happy Birthday, Max," Mitchell said, flashing his sister with a smile.

"Happy Birthday to my favorite bitch," Miguel said as he hugged her.

"You fucking assholes," Max said, laughing as she fell into her brother's hug. "All right, enough sentimental shit, I need to get back to work."

"Henry volunteered to take care of the bar for the next hour, so sit your ass down," Miguel said as Archie cut the cake.

"But, but…"

"No buts, missy. You heard the man, sit your ass down and enjoy yourself for once," Mitchell said, before settling his gaze back on me.

"Same goes for you, Cream Puff."

"What? Oh, I'm not staying, I—"

"Let me buy you a drink."

Archie's backside as he moved around the high top knocked me into Mitchell's space again, and I was starting to get pissed.

"I—" I panicked, trying to think of anything, any sort of excuse to escape this situation. Because between my cock and the heat from embarrassment, and a rather tight space, I was afraid I might literally expire.

"Come on, it's my sister's birthday, and with her in time out, I can guarantee you the drinks will actually be good."

"Fuck you, Mitch!" Maxine bit out, but there was no venom in her voice. Only the sarcasm of an annoyed older sibling.

Mitchell slid his hand behind my back, his palm settling at the dip above my ass, and I felt like I was going to pass out.

"Ar... Archie and I are on the clock," I said, swallowing nervously.

"No, we aren't," Archie quipped. "This was the last job for the day. The shop's already closed up."

Mitchell grinned, and the sight was like hot, melted chocolate ganache over sponge cake.

Fuck.

"Sounds to me like you're pretty free," he said smoothly. "Besides, we do have something to celebrate."

I tried to focus on not melting into a puddle on the floor because everything was converging on me at once.

"I guess..." I said, biting my lip, if only to quell the sudden urge to curse out of panic. "Wait... We do?" I asked. I didn't miss the light stroke of his fingertips along my spine, sending a shiver throughout my entire body.

It was as soothing as it was new.

Different.

I looked at Mitchell, under the bright neon, and something in his dark gaze settled my anxiety.

"Yeah, our partnership," he said, flashing me with a smirk.

"Partnership…" I said the words like I didn't know how to speak English, which was insane.

I could technically speak two languages. English and French.

But under Mitchell's gaze, I could barely speak Caveman.

Mitchell gently pushed against my back, coaxing me to follow him.

I needed to get out of this tight space. I needed to breathe.

"Uh… I guess, one drink wouldn't hurt."

CHAPTER EIGHT

Mitch

"HEY, MITCH, WHAT can I get ya?" Henry drawled from behind the bar.

I'd pulled a couple shifts myself over the years, but I wasn't technically on the M's Place payroll.

But I had to admit, watching Henry sling drinks with ease made me miss the craziness of the weekends, not to mention the tips.

But I didn't miss the drunk assholes throwing up all over the bathroom.

"Going to switch it up from my warm up beer to a rum and coke," I said as I turned toward Penn.

"What about you, Cream Puff? What's your poison?"

Watching Penn's cheeks flush like a freshly steamed tomato every time I called him such only fueled my desire to keep doing it.

He looked pretty fucking cute all flustered, and maybe I was a glutton for punishment.

"I, um, I don't really drink a lot, so I'm not sure—"

"You are old enough to drink, right?" I asked, momentarily wondering if maybe I'd assumed too much, but Penn only blew some fluffy, golden-hued hair out of his eyes with a bratty little huff.

"Of course, I'm old enough. I'm twenty-three."

I smiled as Henry chimed in.

"Can I make a recommendation?" Henry asked as he worked on pouring three beers and passing them out to their owners.

Penn blinked, licking his lips as he turned from me toward Henry.

"That, uh, that would be great."

"If you've got a sweet tooth, the cotton candy martini or the Chateau Ste.

Michelle is pretty good. We've also got Angry Orchard Cider, and if you're really not into cocktails, wine, or beer, there's always White Claw."

I watched as Penn twisted his lips, trying to figure out what he'd go after. My guess was White Claw, so I was surprised when he went for the cider instead.

"Good choice," I said as Henry set about fixing our drinks.

"I think I had it once, but I can't remember what it tasted like," he said with another blush.

"Let me guess, you were one of those guys who blacked out after one crazy hangover-style night and haven't touched the stuff since?"

Penn smirked. "I've never really *blacked* out, even when I have been drunk."

Henry passed us our drinks.

Penn took a sip, puckering his lips.

"When is the last time you were drunk? Or... out in general?" I asked as I stirred my drink first.

Penn shrugged. "I don't know. Toward the end of school, I kinda lost interest. Well, and my friends, too, I guess. But that's to be expected when you break up with someone, I suppose. You become the pariah."

He took a long drink and I noticed his shoulders loosened only a fraction. When he pulled the bottle away, some juice trickled down his lip, to his chin.

My cock twitched immediately at the sight and I let out a grunt of my own as I fought the desire to brush it away with my thumb. So instead, I took a sip of my drink, turning my body slightly away, if only to quiet my cock.

Don't get any bright ideas yet, buddy.

"Fuck 'em," I said, shrugging.

Penn looked at me with surprise. "What?"

"If those people bailed on you because you weren't fucking their friend anymore, they weren't your friends to begin with. I don't know you that well, but from what I do know, I know that you're way better than those kind of superficial assholes."

Penn's eyebrows furrowed as his gaze softened. "Thanks, I think," he said, his voice dropping an octave.

I raised my glass to him. "To new friends. And new experiences."

MITCH

I watched as he raised his bottle, a smile forming on his perfect lips.

"I'll cheers to that," he said as our glasses clinked, my knuckles brushing against the edges of his fingertips.

CHAPTER NINE

Mitch

THE KARAOKE HAD resumed, and I could see Miguel forcing our sister up on stage as the crowd roared.

"Drink up, Cream Puff. Because class starts now."

"Come on, Penn, you have to take a turn!" Archie, Penn's friend, begged.

"Absolutely not," Penn said, shaking his head, his cheeks rosy and his smile damn near contagious.

Nolan chimed in with his rescuing stance, as usual. "Guys, if he doesn't want to, leave him alone."

I had to admit, the pencil pusher was a nice addition to the group. Like Cade, he was a natural empath.

"Thank you," Penn said as Dawson rolled his eyes.

We'd gravitated toward my friends, if only because Cade and company didn't seem to take kindly to me keeping Cream Puff all to myself.

They are worse than a throng of teenage girls.

But there was a part of me that felt like maybe Penn *could* fit in here.

With us.

With *me*.

I watched him drain his third Angry Orchard, his pretty blue eyes sparkling with the glaze of good old-fashioned drunkenness.

At that moment, Will called him to the stage.

Penn's eyes widened in shock, and Archie grinned.

"Archie... No..."

"And leave your adoring fans waiting?" he said with a dismissing wave.

I watched Penn bite his lip, weighing what to do.

I didn't know his friend well—hell, I didn't know Penn well—but from the little I did know, I had a feeling he was just trying to push Penn out of his comfort zone.

New experiences and all.

"I'll go with you," I said definitively, setting my drink on the table.

Penn's gaze shot to me.

"What—"

"Just... let me do the singing, okay. You can just stand there and look pretty."

I watched the blush spread on his cheeks as Archie grinned.

"I—"

"What are you waiting for, get up there!" Archie laughed, taking a sip of his beer as I headed up to take the stage.

I half expected even in my drunken state, that Penn would sit it out and let me take over, so I was thoroughly surprised when I heard his footsteps on the platform behind me.

"All right what did Archie Comics pick out for you to sing?" I drawled as I squinted at the teleprompter as Will queued the song up.

Into The Groove by Madonna.

I cast Penn a glance, raising my eyebrow. "Didn't peg you for a Madonna fan."

But there wasn't enough time for him to answer me. Not when the first few notes came across, and I had to speak into the microphone, "You can dance."

I glanced at Penn, watching his glassy eyes focus on me and then the mic. Deciding if he wanted to be a pretty standby or part of the show.

I continued my first few lines, watching him with intent.

I sang on about getting into the groove, and how a boy had to prove his love.

Penn licked his lips, his gaze flashing from my eyes to my mic. The vibration of the stage and the loud speakers drowned out everything else.

Everything but *him.*

Just focus on me, Cream Puff, you'll be fine.

Suddenly, I wasn't sure if I was convincing him or myself.

Will shouldered him, drawing his attention away as I continued to sing, turning to face the crowd.

MITCH

Over the bright lights, I could see Cade smiling, Weston's arm slung around his neck.

Dawson and Nolan were fighting at the table, while Archie hollered and screamed.

And then I felt a nudge against my arm. I turned, facing bright blue eyes and rosy cheeks that gazed into mine like I had the answers to *everything.*

He sang, his voice clear and strong as he belted out the lyrics about feeling free only when dancing.

I watched as he swallowed harshly, closing his eyes and I picked up where he left off. I lit out the words about locking the door and no one else seeing, watching as Penn opened his eyes and he moved back and forth, finding the rhythm. The groove, as Madonna would say, I guess.

He sang about being tired of dancing by himself, licking his lips as he focused on me.

A smirk spread across my face as I leaned into him, my microphone between us.

I sprang forward with the next line and focused in on his bright blue eyes.

The rest was a blur.

As far as I was concerned, there was no one else in the room but Penn.

We sang in tandem like that, building off of one another until the music faded.

I grabbed him by the back of the neck, pulling him to me as I whispered in his ear, "Good job, Penn." I slapped him on the back appreciatively before handing Will my microphone.

I exited the stage, my body feeling flushed from the heat of our proximity mixed with the harsh stage lights, and my own building desire.

Penn followed after me, calling my name.

"Huh?" I turned around, just as his foot caught on the last step, causing him to pitch forward like a clumsy little lamb.

Despite my inebriation, I reacted first.

I leaned forward, catching him in my arms, preventing his fine ass from complete embarrassment.

The heat that blossomed between us was like an inferno as he looked up at me, eyes glazed with liquor and something else I couldn't place.

His fingertips sank into my heated flesh as he steadied himself.

"Lightweight," I teased as I righted him, but I didn't remove my hands from his hips, and he made no move to stop his fingers from clutching my biceps.

Looking at him in my arms, feeling his grip...

Fuck, I could get used to that look.

My cock twitched as a grunt escaped my throat, mingling with a soft sigh that escaped his.

"Uh, yeah. Guess I'm a mess, huh?" he said wistfully.

I steadied his frame as I shifted us further into the shadows of the empty pool room to let the next contestant—a woman I didn't know—up on the stage.

The shift pulled us into the low-lit corridor adjacent to the game room, which lead toward one of the three emergency exits.

It was close enough to hear the woman wailing on her rendition of Carrie Underwood's *Before He Cheats*, but not so close that we didn't have a modicum of privacy for the moment.

"You're having fun. Fun can be messy sometimes," I said, licking my lips as I focused my gaze on his perfect pout.

I wanted to kiss him.

I wanted to tell him that messy or not, he deserved to have a good time.

I wanted to be the one to show him just all the fun *we* could have.

Together, if he'd give me the chance.

Somewhere in my mind, I knew it was a bad idea. For starters, he was technically a client, and pursuing any sort of romance was unprofessional.

Then there was the whole question about whether or not Penn was even remotely into the idea of any sort of romance or relationship with someone like me.

Because I wasn't a tall, tanned, pretty blonde woman.

I was the furthest thing from that.

But caught up in the shadows, with Penn in my arms, looking like a bedazzled wedding cake with his plush lips and rosy cheeks and glittering eyes...

I couldn't resist.

The words fell out of my mouth without warning.

"I want to kiss you right now," I whispered, my voice catching in my throat.

Penn stood upright, his entire body

stiff as a rod.

"I think... I think I want to kiss you, too... but..."

I reached out, sliding my hand through his damp, sweaty hair.

"But what?" I asked, trying to breathe.

"I've never kissed someone like you... before," he admitted.

In my drunken stupor, I stupidly asked what I already knew. But perhaps I just wanted to hear him say it.

Out loud.

"Like me?" I drawled. "I think I need you to elaborate, Cream Puff."

Penn squeezed my side as his breath shook.

"I mean... I've never kissed a guy," he whispered, licking his lips as he swallowed harshly.

"There's a first time for everything," I said, ignoring all the alarm bells sounding in my head.

I ran my hand down his neck, cradling the back of his head as I used my thumb to nudge his chin up.

Penn fell into me with ease as I brought my mouth to his.

Like he'd been waiting for my kiss all

his life.

His lips against mine were soft and lush, and as sweet as a literal cream puff.

A deep groan escaped him, igniting me like a firework on the fourth of July.

I took his groan as permission to go further, slipping my tongue into his mouth as I pulled him by his hips, moving him closer, brushing my hardness against him.

"Fuck," I whispered, feeling lightheaded as his tongue responded in unison.

The sounds of Will announcing last call rang out, and shattered everything.

Penn broke away, his eyelashes fluttering as he opened his eyes and immediately stiffened once more, pushing away from me.

"Oh fuck, I'm so sorry. I—"

"It's okay, I—"

"I have to go," he blurted, anxiety taking over.

Fuck!

I pushed too hard, I—

"Penn..."

"I... I'm sorry. Thank you for the drinks, but I need to go. I need to go..."

he said, and then he took off like a bat out of hell.

All I could do was watch as he found Archie, and then they headed out the door.

"Fucking asshole!" I snarled, chastising myself as I punched the damn Love Meter machine. It went off with a whir, buzzing and vibrating.

"Shut the fuck up!" I snapped as the meter sounded off, hitting the "Scorching" setting.

"There you are," Cade said as he found me nursing my sore fist.

"Wes and I are headed out. Was wondering if you needed a ride home? I know you came by yourself, but I don't think your brother will care if you leave the car here overnight," he said softly.

I cursed silently, feeling the effects of my alcohol and my shame.

"Yeah, I could use a ride," I said as he settled his hand on my shoulder.

"And maybe while you're at it, you can dig my fucking grave, too."

CHAPTER TEN

Penn

MY HEAD WAS killing me.

I guessed when you didn't go out drinking all that much to begin with though, it was probably ten times worse than you remembered.

Archie, however, was absolutely fine. Or at least, he appeared to be as he waltzed into the shop with a carrier of sweet-smelling coffee.

"Good Morning, Pennington," he sing-songed, making my headache throb and my eye twitch.

"What's so good about it?" I grumbled

as he set the carrier down behind the counter before heading to grab his apron.

While I'd been away at school, Archie and my dad opened the shop most days, but now that I was home, my dad had taken a step back. He and my mom usually came in later now, around mid-morning. Which meant, for the time being, Archie and I had the shop to ourselves.

Archie pulled out a coffee cup and handed it to me with a raised eyebrow.

"Feeling the hair of the dog, eh?" he poked, flashing me with a smirk.

I grabbed the coffee, breathing in its delicious cinnamon-vanilla scent.

Cinnamon Dolce Lattes fix everything.

Except drunken shenanigans.

I popped open the plastic lid, diving into the frothy cream on top, letting the sweetness coat my tongue and soothe my frayed nerves for a moment.

"More like hungover and full of regret," I mewled. "Now I remember why I don't drink."

Archie grabbed his coffee as he leaned back against the back prep counter, imploring me with his steely amber gaze. His naturally tanned skin stood out like fresh-baked gingerbread against the cool marble and cobalt blue.

The sun was only starting to come up, and as such, lit up the inside of the bakery like the gates of heaven.

"Why? Because you get all flirty and handsy when you're drunk?" he teased.

My cheeks flushed with heat at his words, and the memory of last night pushed forth all over again.

Mitchell's hand on my back, his fingertips brushing against mine.

His tongue in my mouth.

My cock awakened at the thought and I gritted my teeth as I focused on breathing.

"It's not like that. I—"

I've never been kissed by any of my girlfriends like... that.

Archie smiled, shaking his head. "You know what they say? Drunk words are sober thoughts. Maybe your actions are more in tune with what you want than you think."

"I'm not... gay, or... or bisexual!" I shouted, feeling on the spot. "I'm straight!"

Some of my cream sloshed over the

side of my cup from my sudden vibration, my voice echoing off the bakery walls.

Even as I said the words through, I felt like something had shifted. Like a volcano erupts or a glacier breaks away, floating apart from its foundation.

Archie *was* gay. Loud, out, and proud gay, and so was Mitchell DeVille. I knew that now, and there was no denying it.

But me... surely I would *know* if I was bi or gay. I mean, a person just knows, right?

I'd *looked* at lots of girls, and found them attractive. But never had I ever popped an instant boner looking at *anyone.*

At least, that was up until I'd seen Mitchell at that wedding.

Or until last night... after we *sang* together... when I fell, and he caught me.

"You trying to convince me, Penn, or yourself?" Archie asked curiously.

"I... I've only ever been attracted to women. I have had, like—"

"Three or four girlfriends? Yeah, how did those relationships work out for you?" Archie asked.

I turned around and instead of

looking at him, I focused on stacking the cooler display.

"That has nothing to do with—"

"It has *everything* to do with it," Archie insisted. "The dick wants what it wants. It does not lie."

"It's not that simple," I refuted.

Archie shrugged as he set to making a fresh batch of cinnamon rolls, the first item on today's calendar prep.

"Don't believe me, watch some porn. You'll figure it out pretty quick."

I huffed in annoyance. "Are you serious? I don't watch porn, like, at all."

Archie snickered. "Then what do you have to lose? Consider it research. If you find yourself all keyed up over tits and ass and tight pussy, then by all means, I will leave you alone about this forever. I'll take your steamy drunk dude make out to my fucking grave," Archie said.

I turned to look at him with a raised eyebrow of my own. "Promise?"

Archie held his hand over his heart. "Promise. But I have a feeling you aren't as straight as you think," he said, turning to roll out the dough, and leaving me to my own devices, just as my parents came in through the door.

What the hell?

They never come in this early anymore.

"Hey, Mom, Dad... Is everything okay?" I asked, suddenly alarmed.

"We need to talk about last night," my dad said, his voice stern, and gruff.

"What?" The blood in my veins ran as cold as a frozen croissant.

A part of me was worried they'd heard us talking, or worse someone might have said something to them. That they might have somehow seen me and my suddenly shifting morals, and that I'd somehow embarrassed not just myself, but my family.

"Well, it's not often you come home so late, and you *did* leave all the lights on," my mom said with a smile as she headed over to grab an apron while my dad settled his arms on the counter.

"The event last night must have been quite a night," he said with a grin, winking at me.

My cheeks reddened again as I stammered.

"Oh, I can assure you, Mr. Baker, it was," Archie said with a giggle.

I shot him a glare. I watched as my

mother rolled the dough smoothly, passing it to Archie to cut and roll.

"What time is the photographer coming today?" she asked, and once again my blood chilled.

I was a popsicle of fear, embarrassment, and curious desire.

It was Monday.

Mitchell would be coming in *today*.

Today, the day after I stupidly got drunk and...

Kissed him.

I kissed a boy, and I—

My cock twitched as the memory filled my brain. Of his warm, soft lips moving hungrily against my own, of the way my entire body—especially my damn cock—responded to his mouth, the sounds he was making.

The hardness I vaguely remember in my pants.

"Um, uh, I think..." I tried to focus on my words, but I felt like I was slowly slipping beneath choppy waves. "I think Mr. DeVille is arriving around noon," I finally said.

Archie snickered in the background, and I turned away.

"Splendid!" my mother said with

excitement.

"I can't wait to see what you two come up with," my father chimed in.

The hours on the clock were like an eternity. Especially, those last fifteen minutes. A part of me wondered if perhaps he wouldn't show. Maybe he, too, was nursing a hangover, and would want to reschedule.

Did I want him to reschedule?

A part of me wanted to avoid looking the man I'd kissed in the eyes, while the other part of me—a larger part—was curious to see him again. Maybe I could apologize, clear the air.

Away from my parents and Archie, of course, which wouldn't be too difficult if I could somehow come up with a guise to get Mitchell alone that wasn't suspicious.

I'd almost sweated myself out of my clothes by the point he actually showed up.

Dressed in tight burgundy jeans and a zebra print button down, his dark hair was gelled back, the lights of the bakery casting a shimmering sheen on his dark locks. Slung across his back was a tripod, and he carried what looked like two giant suitcases. He looked like he was going on a trip to Key West and not a small town bakery to photograph desserts.

Without thinking, I headed toward the door, if only to help him drag in his equipment.

"Hey..." I said as I swooped in to grab the suitcase he gripped in his right hand. "Let me help you with that."

Mitchell smirked, his dark eyes full of mischief and excitement.

"It's good to see you, too, Cream Puff," he said, his voice dark and... *sexy.*

I swallowed harshly as I tried to focus on the task at hand, and not the weird things his deep rumble was doing to me.

For God's sake, my parents are here!

"You must be Mitchell," my father said as he came up beside me, extending his hand. "I'm Samuel Baker, co-owner of Penn's Bakery."

Mitchell's smirk shifted into a much more *polite* smile, his entire demeanor shifting like a chameleon.

"So nice to meet you, Mr. Baker," Mitchell said as he extended his hand.

Panic laced its way through me.

"And this is my wife, and co-owner,

Marissa." He introduced my mom who shook his hand, smiling ear to ear.

"Nice to meet you both," Mitchell said, his voice as saccharine as the buttercream frosting Archie was whipping up for this afternoon's orders.

I forced my legs to move, if only because I needed to get as far away from the Twilight Zone as possible, or I thought I might legit pass out.

Thankfully, my parents had sequestered Mitchell for the moment so I could breathe behind the counter. I dropped his suitcase in front of the display case, figuring it was a good spot. I'd been working on the display practically all day to settle my nerves about this very moment.

Archie smirked at me.

"What's so funny?" I bit out as the oven timer went off for the three tier cake we were working on for Gloria Tanen's fiftieth.

The smell of fresh baked vanilla rounds swept through the air, soothing my senses just a fraction.

"Nothing, nothing at all," Archie snickered as he slid me the buttercream.

I shot him a glare as I kept my back

to my parents and Mitchell, deciding instead to get lost in frosting the cake rounds.

The rest of the day—which was only about four hours or so—I spent avoiding Mitchell.

Which wasn't an easy feat, given the size of our shop. But somehow, I managed to busy myself with Miss Tanen's cake, and spent the last hour doing dishes.

My parents had taken off, and it was just Archie and I. At least, I *thought* it was just Archie and I, until I came around the corner and ran smack into Mitchell, camera still in hand, taking pictures of the marble and cobalt tile, of the back of the counter. He pitched forward a moment, the snap of the shutter going off as he cursed, finding his grounding.

I looked back and forth, expecting to see Archie, but he wasn't in the front.

He never usually left without saying goodbye, so I knew he had to be there somewhere.

Hiding in the freezer maybe?

"Oh, I'm so sorry, I thought you left," I said, startled.

Mitchell set his camera down on the clean counter, raising an eyebrow.

"How could I leave without proper payment?" he said, flashing me a grin.

My cheeks flushed at his insinuation, and I wasn't sure if I should have been offended or not.

"P—payment?" I swallowed, my mind thinking of his plush lips, his tongue in my mouth...

"I believe you *did* say there would be desserts involved in this gig," he said teasingly.

Of course!

I felt like an absolute idiot. He'd offered his services at a discount because I had promised to pitch in some bake shop goodies.

"Yeah... yeah, of course. Uh, so, what, uh, what would you like to take home?" I asked as I slowly ambled backward, away from him.

Mitchell leaned against the back counter, spreading his arms along the ledge. He'd rolled up his zebra print sleeves to the elbow, and the first two buttons on his shirt had been popped.

With the way his dark hair fell in his eyes, and the smirk on his face, I couldn't deny he looked divine.

Just as delicious as any dessert in my display case.

I cleared my throat as I headed toward the case, grabbing a cardboard box and putting it together.

"I can think of one thing that isn't in that case, that I'd *love* to take home," he toyed shamelessly.

I turned from him, my cheeks heating from his words.

What the hell was wrong with me?

Granted, I'd never been the best when it came to flirting, and I usually despised guys who were so cheesy in their pick up lines when it came to women.

No one had ever flirted with me like Mitchell did.

Man or woman.

Something about that made my entire body heat like a bonfire.

Is that what I want?

I wasn't really sure *what* I wanted. I liked Mitchell's words. I thought he was pretty hot, even in a pink zebra print shirt that totally clashed with our clean and crisp aesthetic.

And I had to admit, drunk or not, I liked it when he kissed me.

No, I liked *how* he kissed me. Because no one had ever kissed me like I was some princess in a fairytale.

Like a dragon-slaying knight in shining armor.

"I highly suggest the cinnamon rolls. We make them fresh every day," I said, ignoring his blatant flirtations.

Mitchell didn't press me. He only hummed in understanding as he responded, "Whatever you say, Cream Puff."

I turned around, incensed by the moniker he'd gifted me that first night we'd spoke.

It was hard to believe it had only been a few days ago.

I'd messaged him, and he'd been flirty then, too. I'd just assumed at the time we were joking around, but if I was being honest, it felt easy then, too, talking to him. Letting my guard down.

It was the Internet.

Who didn't say things they wouldn't in person on the Internet?

It didn't mean anything.

It was just... fun, right?

Yet, I couldn't deny every time he called me *Cream Puff*, I actually found I kind of... liked it.

No one had ever really given me a pet name before.

Pet names are for people in relationships, Penn.

You are most certainly not in a relationship with this... man. Photographer.

The photographer you hired to help the bakery get some more focus.

Has the buttercream gone to your head?

"That's not my name," I touted with annoyance, before turning back to the display to fill the box with half a dozen cinnamon rolls.

Where the fuck was Archie?

Why hasn't he broken the case down yet?

Mitchell laughed. "I know. But you make it so easy with those rosy cheeks and those pretty rolling eyes of yours every time I do it," he said.

I rolled my eyes, but he couldn't see me.

At least, I hoped.

"I take it you got everything you needed for the day?" I asked as I set the last cinnamon roll in the box, sealing it.

I turned with the box in my hand to see him zipping up his camera bag and slinging it over his shoulder.

"For the most part, yes. I'll go home, download everything, and start culling and editing. I should have a couple teasers for you by tomorrow," he said, his tone changing from the flirtatious, sexy one to the much more cut, dry, professional one.

The tone he probably used for all his clients.

Because that's what I was.

A client.

Mortification coursed through me once more as I remembered our kiss.

God, he must think I'm a total basket case.

Or a total slut.

Which would be the farthest thing from the truth, but I couldn't deny that the thought—the wonder about what *he* thought about that kiss, about me—was just as nerve wracking as the memory itself.

But I also wasn't the kind of guy who just got drunk and made out with people.

I liked to take things *slow*. Meet

someone for coffee, get to know them, go out on a nice, romantic date, and then, if the moment was right, then I'd kiss them.

And sex?

I didn't even like to fuck until at least three or four dates in, if we even got that far to begin with!

Most of the girls I'd seriously dated never made it past second base, except maybe Amy, and I didn't like to think about the one night stands that left me feeling like a total loser.

Like I'd been used and discarded like a napkin without so much as a companion for breakfast.

The thought of my ill-fated love life left me feeling more than on the spot.

"Oh. Okay. Thanks," I said, clutching the pink box of goodies as I watched him turn his back to me, zipping up his remaining suitcases of equipment.

Mitchell turned to face me, his naturally dark eyes kind, and endearing.

"Of course," he said, his tone softer. "I'll see you tomorrow, Penn."

And with that, he took the goodie box, and headed out the door, leaving me both breathless and feeling guilty as all hell.

How the hell was I going to get through a week of this?

CHAPTER ELEVEN

Penn

IT WAS NEARING nine thirty, and I knew I should go to sleep, but I'd been tossing and turning for at least an hour and couldn't get comfortable.

Partially because I had gone over the past twenty-four hours in great detail. From my arrival at M's Place, to that *kiss*, to Mitchell showing up today, to that weird, charged moment between us before he left.

Including Archie's words.

Maybe you're not as straight as you think, Penn.

I turned on my right side, my gaze falling on my laptop, its screensaver lighting up the darkness of my room like a salacious beacon.

It wasn't that I had anything *against* porn, it just wasn't something I ever experimented with. Mostly because I was afraid my parents would somehow find out and I'd get in trouble. Even when I went away to college, on my own, there was still that veil of taboo-ness that I couldn't shake. I never considered myself a prude by any means, but suddenly, after that kiss, I was questioning a lot more than I ever thought I would.

Maybe, I was overreacting.

Maybe, I was just all keyed up because I was back home in Jasper Springs. Maybe, I was going through some early twenties crisis or something now that I had graduated or something.

Whatever it was, I felt this curious spark inside of me building, cresting with anxiety.

I was twenty-three years old. Surely, I could just watch a little porn. Prove Archie and his speculations wrong.

I crept over to my desk quietly, even

though I knew both my parents were out like a light, and there was no way *anyone* would hear me. Anxiety swelled as I stuffed down the part of me who wanted to turn around and just say we did...

But I was an honest person, if anything, and maybe I was *a little* curious. Being someone who had no idea what the fuck they were doing, I fired up Google like any curious person would do, I'm sure, and googled "where to watch porn" like the complete idiot I was.

I randomly picked a link, hoping it would work.

Immediately, my vision was accosted with women on their knees, cum-stained mouths full of cock, and I shut the lid almost on contact.

Not because it turned me on, because I thought it was kind of gross, actually, but because I had started to wonder if it was a good idea.

"Jesus Christ, Penn, you're a fucking adult, not some hornball teenager. It's research, man, just skim a few videos and call it a night," I said to myself, taking a deep breath before I opened the computer again.

I clicked on the first video again, letting it play as I leaned back in my chair. I didn't *dislike* watching the big, beefy guy shove his cock down the woman's throat, but I wasn't really into her over-acting moans and her sticking her tongue out.

I watched intently as the man's hands slid over his cock, his thumb brushing over the tip of his swollen head. God, the guy was enormous.

Was all porn like that?

Surely, there had to be some regular sized guys out there, right?

Noticing my thoughts were straying, I decided to try something else. A few seconds later, I was viewing a woman being bent over a countertop, with another large, muscled man fucking her from behind.

My cock twitched, as I watched him fist his hand in her hair, watched his slick, thick cock disappear into her ass. I licked my lips, sliding my own hand down beneath my boxers, feeling the smooth skin of my shaft against my palm.

See, Archie, totally straight.

MITCH

I rubbed and tugged slowly, hardening as I continued to watch the man's veins in his arms tighten with every grip of her hair, with every thrust of his cock against her ass. But then it was over in an instant as he pulled out, only to cum all over her, and...

And I was still no closer to coming myself than I had been when I started to watch.

This is ridiculous.

No one actually likes this stuff.

I had half a mind to just close it out, until I saw a gif on the side, something starring a bigger guy, with dark hair and deep eyes, who literally called to me and made me click.

I don't know why or how, and I couldn't even put it into words, but it was like I was just drawn to his aesthetic. He was hot, all tan muscles and wild hair, fiery eyes.

The video that came up on my computer showed him in the shower, the water running down his defined chest in rivulets and my cock sprang to attention.

There he was, standing there alone, running his large hands over his chest, through dark, chestnut hair, down his abdomen. The curve of his golden-skinned ass, the definition of his muscles... I watched as he tilted his head back, running his hand down to his...

I swallowed, hard, as I watched him grip his thick, pink cock, tugging at his length as he *groaned.*

It was like a train wreck. I literally could not pull my gaze away, and I didn't *want* to.

I licked my lips again as I pulled at my own cock, feeling myself harden again with renewed vigor.

I watched him lean his hand against the tile, thrusting into his hand slowly.

Watched as his cock disappeared into his slippery, wet hand.

Then he looked up. The sound of the shower door opened, and I tensed. I don't know what I was expecting, but an average sized, blond male, who looked to be about in his early twenties, stepped in. His body wasn't as defined as the tall, dark, and handsome man pleasuring himself in the shower.

In fact, golden boy's body kind of reminded me of my own. Soft around the edges, but trim enough that I had *some* shadow of a six pack.

Okay, well, technically, I had fallen off the workout train after I broke up with Amy, on account her friends were gym rats who practically lived at the university rec center.

I watched in curiosity as the smaller man came up behind the star of the show, who never broke character or turned around. I watched as golden boy lathered his hands up and down the man's body, fingers splayed across muscles. Something in the way he touched him, smoothly, lazily, caused my cock to twitch as I watched him trail his lips over the other man's neck, his fingers brushing along the other man's hand.

My own hand built its rhythm as I felt my orgasm building deep in my balls, my cock stiff as a slab of marble. A fresh bead of precum dribbled from my slit and spread along my fingers. I let out a shaky breath as understanding dawned on me.

I liked what I saw.

For the first time in a long time, I felt connected to myself. I was enjoying something I often thought of as a nuisance or a chore.

My breathing hitched as I watched the golden boy drop to his knees, parting the man's legs as he ran his *tongue* along the man's ass, and then...

His fingernails dug into the man's flesh as deep groans left his throat, and the man he was accosting—no, *eating out*—came without warning.

And so did I.

My breath shook as I cursed, my release coating the inside of my hand and my boxers. My cock pulsed, and my head fell back against the back of the chair, my eyes fluttering closed as I rode out the waves of the most *intense* orgasm I'd ever felt.

And when it was over, I opened my eyes, and the truth hit me like a ton of bricks.

Archie was right.

Maybe I wasn't as straight as I thought.

And that changed everything.

CHAPTER TWELVE

Mitch

MY ALARM WENT off far too early for my taste. Especially, since I'd been up until at least one in the morning working on Giselle and Aaron's massive photo cull and edits.

I had promised Penn that I would have some teasers, or at least some good raw images for him to check out, but I'd completely forgotten about the wedding of the century sitting at home on my computer.

But I was a man of my word, and come hell or high water, I was *not* going to show up to Penn's Bakery without *something* for my little Cream Puff to view. After all, he *did* send me home with some delicious cinnamon rolls.

I slammed my hand against the incessant alarm on my phone, groaning as I tumbled out of bed. Penn's parents had informed me that Penn and his friend slash co-worker, Archie, usually opened the shop around five am, which wasn't my favorite time to get up, but being as the sunrises in Jasper Springs always looked best first thing in the morning, for the shot I wanted to get, I knew I was going to have to be an early riser.

If only I would have quit on time last night, instead of going through pictures from the bakery.

I'd managed to capture a few of Penn, as well as Archie and his parents doing their thing.

I couldn't help as I culled and edited the good stuff, that I let myself get a little lost in the details. When you're a photographer, you see everything. People's flaws, the scar on their left cheek from when they fell when they were six, the wrinkles at the corners of their eyes, even the tiniest frayed and static hair. Part of my job is to cover up those flaws. But in contrast to that, my job isn't so much about making someone beautiful with an airbrush. It's about finding the beauty in the things that already exist.

And let me tell you, zoomed in at 400%, there was not a flaw on Mr. Perfect as far as my trained eyes could see.

I got lost in the smoothness of his skin, the thickness of his eyelashes. The look of utter concentration on his face as he worked diligently on his cake and avoided me like the plague.

I'd thought maybe he regretted what happened between us. That I'd been an idiot and pushed where I shouldn't have.

But then when we were all alone, with no one else to be seen, he seemed less cold.

It was almost as if he *wanted* to open up, wanted to explore whatever was forming between us.

And as much as I knew it was probably a bad idea, I couldn't deny I wanted to explore the unknown, too, even though I knew it might hurt me in the long run.

I jumped in the shower, letting the hot water soothe my sore muscles. Most people didn't think about the physical demands of my job.

I didn't have an assistant, and I never had. I was a one man show, and as such, only I was responsible for my equipment, my car, my happy clients.

But I'd be lying if I said it didn't come with its own set of problems, too.

Including the sore back and muscles.

God, I'm not even thirty yet, what the fuck?

I lathered up the soap, taking my time to wash up, if only because I was tired and hated early mornings.

I ran my hands along my body, working up a good layer of suds. I wasn't the bulkiest guy at the gym by any means, but I was no stick either. After all, you've got to possess some strength to carry heavy ass equipment to weddings and what not.

As my hands made their way to my balls, I closed my eyes and breathed in the relaxing citrus and pine scent. My cock twitched against the back of my hand, and I knew it was better to just take care of myself rather than wait for my damn erection to die down on its own.

I took my cock in my hand like I normally did, pulling and tugging on my shaft until I found the rhythm that I wanted.

Usually, I can just rub one out without too much thought, but for some reason, my brain wanted to cause me more problems.

Because instantly, as I thrust my cock in my hands, *his* image came to mind.

Bad idea, Mitch.

Don't go there.

I knew I shouldn't.

But it was just a fantasy, and I was alone, so what did it matter?

At least that was what I told myself, at the time.

Instead of fighting what felt natural, I let the thoughts bloom.

The memory of his tongue in my mouth, the deep groan that escaped his lips when he kissed me.

His hardness against mine.

Fuck!

Sticky moisture beaded at my slit,

and my hips picked up their pace. I knew it wouldn't be long.

The thoughts mingled with the memories as I imagined his soft, plush lips along my heated skin, his warm tongue licking me along my shaft, until he wrapped his lips around my swollen head, and...

"Fuck!" I barked as I fell forward against the tile, bracing myself as I came suddenly.

My stomach muscles spasmed as my cock pulsed and I tried to catch my breath, watching my release circle the drain. I tugged my cock, working to empty the remains as my muscles started to soften, leaving me with a sense of euphoria.

Fuck, how the hell am I going to make it through seven days of this, if I can barely handle twenty-four hours?

CHAPTER THIRTEEN

Mitch

WHEN I FINALLY arrived at Penn's Bakery at six oh three in the morning, I was feeling much more relaxed.

I'd stopped at the Starbucks on the way, fully intent to grab myself a coffee, but decided to on a whim grab Penn one, too.

After all, what was a day spent with baked goods without a proper cup of coffee?

I didn't know the guy all that well, but given he worked with sugar, and considered himself a cream puff man, I'd opted to get him a Cinnamon Dolce Latte. Then, because I'm not a complete asshole, I tossed on a Chai Tea Latte for Archie. I remembered him going on about how he was obsessed with them the other night at M's Place.

It seemed like a good idea.

I walked across the street, nodding at the daylight warriors who were also leaving their cars and the others who were starting to filter in on the street to park and head to their jobs.

I opened the door to see Archie stocking the case, Penn behind the counter, wiping everything down.

"Good Morning!" I called out, catching his attention.

Penn looked up, his eyes widening in shock as if it was Groundhog Day or something.

I approached him, carrying the carrier of drinks in one hand, dragging my suitcase with my tripod strapped to my back. I'd taken to wearing the camera around my neck for the moment.

I'm sure I looked every bit the weary traveler at that time of morning.

"Here, let me help you with that," Penn said as he threw down his rag, exiting from behind the counter to come around to my aid.

I couldn't help but smile at his actions. He truly was just as sweet as the delicacies he carried in his shop.

"I come bearing gifts," I said as he grabbed the suitcase.

"Gifts?" he said, raising an eyebrow.

With my spare hand, I checked the labels, before handing him his drink.

"Cinnamon Dolce Latte for the Cream Puff, Chai Tea Latte for the pain in the ass, and Tuxedo Mocha with an extra shot of espresso for the photographer," I said, flashing a grin.

Archie came around to receive his drink, smiling. "Thanks, man," he said as I nodded.

"Yeah, don't get too used it. I needed the caffeine and my mama didn't raise an asshole." I flashed him a grin.

Penn chuckled as he took a sip of his drink, his eyelashes fluttering as he moaned in satisfaction.

The sound went straight to my cock, and the memory of my fantasy this morning resurfaced.

Not now!

"God, I swear these things will fix

anything," Penn said as Archie nonchalantly grabbed the suitcase, whistling as he pulled it back behind the counter to put it in the office no doubt, like he had yesterday.

Which left Penn and I alone for the moment.

"It's like six am, Penn. What do you need to fix already? The day hasn't even started."

Penn sighed, running his fingers along the heated cardboard.

"If you only knew..." His voice was wistful, yet sarcastic.

Clearly whatever was bothering him was stressing him out.

"Try me."

Penn sipped his drink again, twisting his lips as he gazed up at me as if contemplating what to say.

Or rather, *how* to say it. But he thought better of it.

He sighed, shaking his head as he murmured. "Stupid fucking porn."

The adult in me knew I should probably leave it alone, whatever it was clearly was none of my business.

But the immature asshole in me could not very well leave well enough alone, and of course, I steamrolled through that admission like I was scoring a touchdown.

"Really, Cream Puff? Your panties all in a bunch because the WiFi cut you off too early or something?" I teased.

"Oh my God! I didn't just say that out loud! Oh my God!" His cheeks turned pink, and I couldn't help but laugh.

I reached out, setting my free hand on his shoulder. "It's okay, sweetheart, it happens to the best of us," I taunted him, flashing him a wink.

His cheeks reddened as he groaned. "I am so fucking bad at this!" he said, turning around, and practically *running the other way.*

"Bad at what?" I called out, as he huffed, scampering behind the counter.

I swung my tripod off my shoulders, setting my coffee down on one of the tables in front of the big bakery window. The sun had started to peek up and I knew I didn't have much time to get the shot I wanted.

"Nothing!" he called out from behind the counter, and I couldn't help but smile, hearing the embarrassment in his voice.

He looked so damn cute when he blushed like that.

I unzipped the tripod, hurrying to set it up to get my shot. I'd just gotten everything set up when the light hit the window, like a firework. I knew once I got the photos downloaded for the day, seeing those bright blue letters amidst the sparkling sunrise, it would be stunning.

And just like most things in life, it was over in a literal flash. I'd stopped the moment, even if only for a fraction, embedded in photography forever.

As I disassembled the camera from the tripod stand, I had to wonder if that wasn't some weird metaphor for my life.

I was always waiting for the right moment to capture, but in doing so what had slipped through my fingers?

I turned to look at Archie and Penn, working in unison to one another as the first customer came through the door.

"Good Morning!" Penn said cheerily, his smile stretching from ear to ear.

"Oh, Penn, you're home!" The woman squealed as she ran up to the counter to give him a hug.

I knew most people in town, and she

did look familiar, but that was also the rough part of this job. Everyone looked familiar, but rarely anyone stood out.

Not like Penn does, with his bright eyes and pretty smile, and his golden boy aura.

I instinctively framed them in my viewfinder, zooming in as she hugged him tightly. The smile on his face was genuine, soft, and caring.

This woman wasn't just a customer to him.

She was family.

Click, snap, click.

His gaze flashed up at me a second later, noticing my observation.

And for a moment, I thought he smiled at me, too, but that would be crazy, right?

I lowered my camera as he held out his arms, sliding his right one around her back.

"Got in last week, Miss Reynolds, and I've just been playing catch up. You know how it is."

I watched as he helped her to the counter and Archie popping in with a, "Hey, Miss R!"

"Archibald, it is always a pleasure,"

she said with a chuckle.

"What can I get you this morning, ma'am?" Penn drawled, the saccharine sound of his voice like something out a romance movie.

He really was prince fucking charming.

"Oh, I'll just have an order of those amazing cinnamon rolls for the boys at the office. You know how men love their sweets! Can't get 'em to work without a little food motivation," she said, flashing a grin.

I couldn't help but chuckle at her words as I continued to watch the event unfold through my camera. This was going to be gold for his campaign, no doubt.

An idea shot through me, and I decided to file it away, with the hope that it may help later, after I'd gotten things edited, and after I finished the wedding of the century.

CHAPTER FOURTEEN

Mitch

THE DAY HAD been more than eventful. Not only was the bakery packed from seven am until at least three, but the phone was continuously ringing off the hook with orders.

I'd just zipped up my suitcase, when Penn came around the corner, wiping his hands on his apron.

"Oh, I'm sorry, I didn't realize you were in here," he said, moving to turn around.

"If you have a minute, I can show you those teasers from yesterday?" I asked, unzipping the front flap where I stored my USB drive.

"Oh... I.... I mean, you don't *have* to. I—"

"I promise I won't bite," I said with a smirk, noting how Penn's shoulders loosened, how his eyes dipped to my lips as he licked his own. "Unless you want me to, that is," I teased, testing him out.

I turned the USB in my hand nervously, watching his face, holding my breath.

Pen nodded with a sigh.

"Right, I mean, it's just pictures."

"Right, just... photos," I said as I plugged my USB drive in, bringing up the set of four images I'd worked on last night.

Penn slowly took a few steps forward, his shoulder brushing mine in the small office.

That close I could smell the spray or body wash he'd used. Cinnamon and cloves, mixed with cedar and pine. I fought to breathe him in, acutely aware of his proximity.

I pulled up the first image, one of him and his mom working on a cake.

"Wow, this is really great," he said

softly. "My mom's going to love this."

A soft smile played at my lips. "Can totally see the resemblance."

I watched Penn's cheeks tinge pink, making my heart skip a beat.

"You don't take compliments very well, do you?"

Pen flashed his pretty blue eyes at me. "Why do you say that?"

I watched as he tucked some stray blond hair behind his ear.

"Well, for starters, you blush every time I give you one."

Penn's gaze flashed to mine once more as he chewed his lip.

"I guess I'm just not used to good looking guys complimenting *me*. Usually, I'm the one dishing out sweet nothings, you know," he said, his voice small.

I wanted more than anything to wrap my arms around him and pull him into my lap, tell him to hell with everyone else.

As far as I was concerned, he was damn perfect.

But the sincerity in his voice called to something much deeper than my need to worship and adore Prince Charming.

What Penn *needed* was acceptance.

He needed the space to feel safe and comfortable in who he was, in figuring it all out.

Maybe I wasn't cut out for *this.*

Maybe I was just playing with fire.

But as I looked at Penn's bright blue eyes, the computer monitor shining an ethereal light on him, I knew it didn't matter what I wanted.

I'd be whatever Penn needed me to be.

"That's because most men are afraid saying nice things means they're soft."

Or gay, but we all know niceness and penchant for dick are not mutually exclusive.

"Thanks," he said, a ghost of a smile on his lips.

"You're welcome, Cream Puff," I said with a grin as I cycled to the next photo. I didn't miss the way his eyes lit up when I did so, and that was all I needed.

For the moment, anyway.

"I love the angle of this," he said as he illustrated with his long, lithe fingers toward the cake on screen. "It looks like something that should be in a magazine," he drawled, turning to me once more. "You're really good, you know that?"

Unlike Penn, I could take a compliment, but when it involved my work, I was my worst critic. But as I looked at the image, at the awe on his face, I felt seen in a way I hadn't before.

"I mean, a good photographer should be able to photograph anything within ten feet of their vision, so..."

"Really?" Penn said, his tone much lighter.

I nodded, swiveling in the chair as he crossed his arms, raising an eyebrow at me.

"Yeah. Really. That's, like, photography 101."

"What would you photograph here?" he said, twisting his lips.

The bakery office was pretty tight, and the shelves were stacked with supplies, the desk full of binders and paperwork among knick-knacks. Even the chairs, including the one I was sitting in, were dated. Much more so than the outside of the bakery.

But as far as I was concerned, there was only one thing worth photographing in my vision.

And he was a lot closer than ten feet.

I smirked as I leaned back in the chair, spreading my legs as I cast him a dark glance.

While I may have had my own awkward moments in middle and high school with my sexuality, as an adult, I felt like I had a good handle on my own sex appeal.

And judging by the way Penn's pupils dilated, I knew he was susceptible.

"You," I said confidently.

Penn swallowed harshly. "Me? Seriously? I'm a mess."

I chuckled at his golden hair, all disheveled, at the apron covered in cake batter, dried icing, and chocolate.

At those perfect, pristine blue eyes, and pouty lips.

God, he was so fucking *pretty*.

"It's the little details of imperfection that make things perfect."

I could tell we were starting to venture into flirty, heated tension territory, and I didn't want to overwhelm the guy too much, so I quickly said, "What about you? Cream Puff? What would you photograph?"

Penn furrowed his eyebrows as he looked around the space, taking it all in, thinking.

It was cute as all hell.

He framed his fingers like a lens, looking at me through them.

"You," he said firmly. "All spread out like a GQ model."

It was my turn to blush, the heat rising in my cheeks even as I let out a dark chuckle.

"Only, I'd add some chocolate, and some cheesy tagline, like..."

"One bite and you'll be on your knees?" I offered, with a laugh.

Penn's eyebrows shot up as his cheeks flushed scarlet, and he laughed.

"I mean, that is a pretty solid tagline," he said.

"Oh, and for shits and giggles, we could add a tub of chocolate frosting in between my legs." I laughed.

Penn chuckled, shaking his head. "Are you always this... this..."

"What?" I asked through my laugh.

"Scandalous?" he said grinning.

"Oh, Penn, this isn't scandalous. This is me being polite."

Penn bit his lip, looking me over for a moment before speaking.

"We make a good team, don't we?" he

asked softly.

I cocked my head to the side. "I think we do."

Silence befell us, and I was certain we weren't talking about cakes and goodies anymore.

I waited for a moment to see what he would do. If he would act on whatever desire or thoughts he was having, but he only stood there, stiff as a board.

Afraid.

How can I show you that you don't have to be afraid, Penn Baker?

That was the moment his father decided to come into the already tight office space.

"Dad! I thought you and mom left..."

"Your mother forgot her sweater," Mr. Baker said, rolling his chocolate eyes.

In the office, up close to Penn, I could see similarities, but Penn looked more like his mother with his complexion, his golden hair, and his ocean blue eyes. His father was a pretty large and bulky framed man with olive skin and jet-black hair. It was like night and day, though Penn shared the same jaw-line, the same thick eyelashes, and the same shape of mouth.

He truly was the best of both of his parents. A beautiful subject.

"There it is!" his father said as he moved to grab the sweater draped over the chair I was sitting in.

"Oh, I'm sorry!" I said as I grabbed it, handing it to the man.

Penn looked more than flushed. He looked like he was going to pass out.

Of course, he must be worried his dad saw something...

"Penn and I were just going over some photos I took yesterday, if you'd like to take a look," I offered, speaking as professionally and curtly as possible.

Penn caught my glance and I tried to shoot him a reassuring smile.

It's okay, I got this. Your secret is safe with me.

"Oh, that's all right, I can look at them later. We're headed out for the night to visit our friends in the city, and we really need to get going."

"Fair enough. Have a lovely evening!" I said sweetly as his dad slung the sweater over his shoulder, hugged his son, and made his way out of the office.

When I was certain he was gone, I spoke, pulling Penn from his frozen state.

"When's your next event?" I asked, deciding to change the subject so my little Cream Puff could breathe easier.

"What?" he said, blinking, shaking his head. Coming back down to Earth from where his thoughts had taken him...

God only knew what was going through his mind.

"Your next big event? You know, like a wedding, or a party, or..."

"Oh, uh..."

"I was hoping I could get some shots of you and Archie out in the field," I said as I pulled the USB out of the computer.

Penn moved next to me once more, checking the calendar on the wall beside me. That close, I could feel the heat rolling off of him.

He was practically sweating.

The motion pulled his shirt up on the side, exposing the sliver of perfect, golden skin, making my cock twitch.

Fuck, now is really not the time!

"Purely business related, Penn," I said, hoping it would settle his anxiety, and also to quiet my damn cock with a mind of its own.

It wasn't like I was asking him on a date or anything. It was just... business.

Right?

"Right..." he said, licking his lips. "I, uh, have an event tomorrow night. Near the city," he said quietly.

"Time?"

"Six."

"Cool. If it's okay with you, I can meet you and Archie at the event?"

I watched his eyebrows furrow. "You mean, you wouldn't be coming into the shop tomorrow morning?"

I didn't miss the hint of disappointment there, but I didn't want to read into it. No, I couldn't afford to get hopeful.

Even though I wanted to believe it was because he wanted to see *me*.

"Well, if you have an event, those are usually a couple hours, right?"

Penn nodded. "Yeah, I guess so."

"I'll need time to edit what I took today, plus I still have a boatload of photos to go through from Giselle and Aaron's wedding."

"Right, right. I'm not your only gig, I get it," he said, and I frowned.

I hadn't wanted him to think I was

brushing him off, or that I didn't care about this gig.

"Penn..."

"No, it's fine, I get it. Uh, yeah, you can meet me at The Robin. Six o'clock."

I nodded in response as I packed up the USB once more, and grabbed my suitcase.

"It's a date. See you tomorrow, Penn."

CHAPTER FIFTEEN

Penn

I'D BEEN TO The Robin a couple times in my life, mostly for events. My parents said in the past it used to be a little local style tavern, but after it changed hands with new owners, they completely redesigned the space to have a more modern feel. Though some of the original design was still intact, such as the deep, mahogany walls and the blue tile floor with the specks of silver all throughout.

Archie and I took turns unloading the van. While weddings were our bread and butter, I personally loved the special occasion or milestone parties like this one, for Tracy Lewis's fiftieth. There was just something that pulled at my heartstrings about having a big birthday party with your closest friends, all decked out.

When her friend called to place the order for the cake, I was given a few suggestions. Black, gold, and silver was the color scheme, and they asked that the cake have a "Gatsby vibe".

So of course, I went all out on the theme, adding little silver painted champagne bottles that spilled out large edible pearls and jimmies, cascading down the three tiers.

Just as I gripped my hand around the box, I slipped.

"Fuck!" I said, thanking my lucky stars I didn't drop the cake.

"Need a hand?" a familiar voice asked.

I looked over my shoulder to see Mitchell, once again dressed in some flashy island print shirt, his dark hair gelled back to expose his flawless olive skin.

My gaze roved over him, down to his tight, black jeans, and my cock twitched in my own.

Fucking hell.

"Uh... yeah..." I stammered, like an absolute idiot.

How was it that every time this guy walked in the room, my brain took a vacation?

Mitchell slung his camera around his neck around to his back as he helped lift the other end of the box.

"Okay, go slow," I said.

Mitchell smirked. "Always."

Thankfully, I could hide my blush behind the box as my insides twisted at the tone of his voice.

I'd never really appreciated anyone's voice before. But there was something about the way Mitchell spoke, even when he was being flirty as all hell that was just... soothing. Relaxing.

I could fall asleep to that voice.

Mitchell led me in through the door, pausing to ask if I was okay every few steps, until we'd reached our destination in the reserved room.

The place was decorated with Gatsby-twenties style decorations, and all the mingling partygoers were dressed in costume.

"Shit, I feel overdressed as fuck," Mitchell said as we set the cake box down.

"I mean, I knew there was a theme, but they didn't mention there would be costumes," I said as I worked closely on separating the box from the cake itself.

I could hear Mitchell clicking away. Compared to my black button down and dark jeans, he definitely looked better than I did.

Seriously, I wished I could wear prints like that, but I'd just look like a reject from the eighties. Mitchell looked like some smooth model from South Beach.

"Looks good," Archie said as he started to unfasten the tape on the box. We still had one more box to get—the box of sheet cake that would be in the back for traying up and serving the party.

Most of our three-tier cakes had a real top layer, but the bottoms were fake. Partially to keep down on the amount of cake related incidents in transport, but also because of cost. It was a lot cheaper for our clients to order what was essentially a small cake for the guest of honor and a large sheet cake that could feed a hundred people easier and for less.

"There's still the sheet cake..." I started as Archie waved me off.

"I got this. Why don't you go grab something to eat. I know you've got to be starving."

My shoulders loosened as my stomach rumbled. He was right, I was hungry. Mostly because I'd spent all day sweating over tonight.

It was weird to walk into the shop that morning, without seeing Mitchell. Even after just a few days, I'd gotten used to his being around, and I kind of missed him.

"Are you sure?" I protested, but Archie only glared at me.

"Go. We've got plenty of time before we have to tie this up and get it ready."

Mitchell shrugged. "You don't have to tell me twice," he said as he cocked his head toward the main dining room, near the bar. "I haven't had more than a cup of coffee and a cinnamon roll today," he said as I reluctantly followed and Archie headed for the doors.

"Busy day for you, too, I take it?" I

asked, glancing around the dining room. It wasn't packed by any means, but there was a good handful of people dining, and sitting at the bar. Mitchell walked up and grabbed a menu off the bar, taking a seat at one of the open stools.

I followed suit, if only because I didn't know what else to do.

"Yeah, weddings are usually a lot in general. Just hours and hours of adjusting lighting and cropping out family members making weird faces and... This is probably boring the shit out of you."

I shook my head. "No, not at all. I think it's interesting. I mean, I get that talent only gets you so far. The rest is just hard work, right?"

Mitchell smirked. "It's not work if it's something you love."

"No, it's still work," I said with a laugh. "But it's a *labor* of love."

Mitchell passed me the menu as he asked, "Did you always want to be a baker?"

I scanned the menu, my gaze settling on an appetizer platter full of hot wings, fried cheese sticks, and potato skins, and my mouth watered.

I shrugged as I set the menu down. The bartender came over, took our orders—my platter, Mitchell's steak flatbread, and two cokes—just as Archie came in with the giant box.

"Hold on, let me—"

"I got it, Penn!" Archie touted as he wobbled around the corner.

Mitchell reached out to steady him.

"Tell you what, you wait here for our food, and I'll help Archie get this back to the kitchen, okay?" Mitchell offered, getting up from his stool.

I wanted to protest, but the look he shot me had my cock twitching and my ass frozen to the seat.

No one had ever looked at me like *that.*

"Uh... okay..." I stuttered as Archie and Mitchell walked off.

"What the hell am I doing?" I asked myself out loud, when they were out of earshot. The bartender slid our cokes to me, his gaze judgmental.

I guess I'd be judgy of a guy sitting at the bar talking to himself, too.

Everything felt so different.

I'd been out with Archie, and my ex-girlfriends, plenty of times. It wasn't like I didn't *know* how to go out *once in a while*, have a little fun.

But something about Mitchell felt different than it had with everyone else. I knew we were working, technically, but there was an ease about him, that I just wanted nothing more than to sit down, eat some junk food, and have a beer and *laugh.*

When he returned, he smiled. "Good job holding the fort down," he said with a wink.

"Please, all I did was watch the bartender pour the coke from the fountain."

"The party should be arriving in like twenty, Archie said. So we've got more than enough time to eat and work."

I scooted toward him, if only because I wanted to get closer to the bar.

"I kinda always knew I'd be a baker. My mom, she was always baking at home, letting me help her. When she opened the shop, I just knew it was where I'd end up. It was my home away from home."

"That must have been amazing. Sharing the passion with someone else who gets it."

"Your family doesn't get photography?" I asked quizzically.

Mitchell laughed. "No, they do not. I mean, the hospitality and restaurant business is way different. I'm basically self-employed, so I *am* my business. If I'm not chasing the clients, posting on all the channels, doing the thing and keeping my name in the forefront... then I'm not working."

I guess I never really thought about how hard that would be, being as I've basically been brought up and raised to take over the family business. I could only imagine how scary it was to *be* your business. A one man show.

"Still, you're like the *top* photographer in Jasper Springs. You're practically small town famous."

"Not as famous as Dawson Richards, Mr. March," he joked.

I didn't remember much of my conversations with Mitchell's friends from the other night, including the firefighter, but I did recall they all seemed pretty chill and cool.

I wouldn't mind us all hanging out together again in the future.

Somewhere in my gut, I knew that was some sort of sign.

Some inkling of destiny, but at the time I fought to ignore it.

"I don't know, I think you're pretty hot," I said, realizing the instant I said it, that I didn't just *think* it.

My cheeks burned like a five alarm fire as embarrassment flooded me and I hid my face in my hands.

"Oh my God, I am so sorry. I can't believe I—"

Mitchell let out the deepest laugh, and within seconds I felt, warm, soft hands pulling at mine. The touch sent a shiver up my spine.

It felt... different.

His warm palm against my skin was smooth, relaxing, and surprisingly gentle.

He pulled my hands down slowly, his dark gaze holding mine. I was acutely aware of the tension between us, and the fact that I couldn't take my eyes off his lips.

Lips I remembered just how they felt against my own.

"Penn, listen..."

Oh God, this is the part where I

completely fuck everything up.
This is my early life crisis.
"Uh..."

"You don't have to be afraid of what you feel. With me, I mean. I'm not going to judge you. I..."

I watched as he swallowed, his gaze softening as he set my hands in my lap, his thumb brushing over my knuckles faintly, as if he too were afraid.

And for some reason, that made me feel better. More at ease.

"I know how... *confusing*... things can be when you're trying to figure it all out."

My blood chilled as I prepared for his rejection.

Why did I care if he rejected me?

It's not like this was a date, and he wasn't my—

Wait, did I want him to be my—

"I know what it feels like to question things and second guess yourself. But I need you to know it's okay to feel what you feel. To be who you are. If that's a guy who likes tall, pretty blondes..."

I frowned, the memory of Amy interrupting us at the coffee shop resurfacing.

Mitchell smirked. "Or a guy who

likes..."

"Tall, dark, and handsome photographers?" I gulped, feeling strangely emboldened by his words.

I watched the grin on his face widen, and his own cheeks tinge pink.

"I like you, Penn. But I don't want you to think I'm pushing or being too forward or..."

"I just... this is all new for me. I like you, too, I think. I just—"

Mitchell's thumb ran rhythmically over my knuckles, making me feel like everything was going to be okay.

Somehow, this bright, new world of feeling and attraction didn't seem so scary.

Because when I looked at him, I felt *seen.*

Like for the first time in my life, someone *got me.*

My gaze dipped to his lips, then his dark, fiery eyes.

"What is it?" he asked.

"I..." I swallowed, wondering if I really *could* be honest with him.

And myself.

Saying it out loud meant it was real.

That the reality I once knew was over.

I'd shatter my own glass ceiling, but maybe... maybe that's what I needed.

To emerge from my cocoon and embrace the unknown.

I squeezed his hand as I took a deep breath.

It was now or never.

I scooted closer, the motion putting me right between his legs. "I kind of want to kiss you," I whispered.

Mitchell smiled, and it was soft. Sweet.

His eyes glittered in the amber light of the bar. "Then kiss me," he said, his voice dark and gravelly. "I won't stop you."

My entire body felt alive with fear, desire, and curiosity. It wouldn't be the first kiss we shared, but up until that moment, I'd rationed it was the alcohol that pushed me to act so brazenly the last time.

But there was no denying the truth, when without an ounce of alcohol in either of our systems, the desire was just as maddening, just as overwhelming as it had been before.

And that changed everything.

I slowly leaned into his space, my

breath shaking as I did so.

Mitchell met me halfway, cocking his head to the side, his breath low and heavy as he whispered, "I'll never stop you."

I closed the distance between us, ghosting my lips against his, closing them against his bottom lip. His lips were soft against mine, not rough or harsh, and he stayed still as a statue, waiting.

Waiting for me to make the jump.

I settled my free hand on his neck, feeling his pulse beneath my fingertips, the rush of blood and warmth. I moved my lips slowly against him, acclimating to the taste and feel of him. When I was drunk, all I could remember was the *heat*. His tongue accosting mine, the deep groans that left our throats, and our raging alcohol-fueled boners.

But this kiss wasn't like that at all. I gripped his neck a little tighter, sliding my fingers back in his hair as I probed his lips with my tongue.

And then the throat clearing "ahem" of the bartender with our food reminded me where we were, and what we were really doing. I broke away, heat flushing my cheeks.

"Hungry?" he asked with the sexiest grin I think I've ever seen.

"Um... starving," I said as I turned back in my chair toward my leaning tower of appetizers, feeling a new sort of hunger that had nothing to do with wings and mozzarella sticks.

CHAPTER SIXTEEN

Penn

"I KNOW THIS probably sound cliché, but... I had a really good time tonight," I said as I helped Mitchell finish packing up his equipment in his truck.

I didn't miss the smirk on his lips, or the way my cock responded.

I was *so* out of my league.

"I had a good time, too, Cream Puff. In fact, that's probably the most fun I've had at work in a long time."

The smile that formed on my face was irrefutable.

"Really?" I managed to squeak out,

my cheeks heating.

Mitchell nodded. "You know," he started as he tossed his tripod in the trunk of his black Jeep Cherokee. "We could do this again. Outside of work, I mean."

His tone was even, careful. Almost as if he was afraid he'd say the wrong thing.

My eyebrows furrowed as I realized what he was asking.

"You mean, like a... date?" I said cautiously.

Mitchell nodded. "Well, unless you just want it to be a friendly hangout. It can be whatever you want it to be."

His voice was solid, unwavering.

And I think that was the moment I realized I was in over my head.

Because the idea of going on a *date* with Mitchell sounded like a really good idea.

So I sucked in a deep breath, and said, "Yes." I nodded, tasting the word on my tongue. "Yes, I think I'd like that. To go on a... date. With you."

If my cheeks were pink before, I could tell by the heat ransacking my body, they were probably tomato red now. I had never felt so on the spot in my life, waiting for someone to respond. Anxiety and panic flooded me. But the grin that spread on Mitchell's face soothed all of that.

"How does after work tomorrow sound?"

CHAPTER SEVENTEEN

Penn

THE WHOLE DAY I felt like I was on pins and needles. For starters, with Mitchell nearly ten feet away most of the day, it was hard to ignore our impending...

Date.

I'd agreed to go on a date with a guy, and I'd be lying if I said I wasn't nervous. Not because I'd never hung out one on one with another man before, but because I didn't know what the protocol was. I knew I wasn't like most guys in general when it came to the women I'd dated, but then again, Mitchell didn't seem like most guys either.

There was something about him, something I couldn't quite put my finger on.

"You're going to run a hole in the ground, Penn," Archie said, cornering me in the stock room. "What is up with you today?"

I avoided his gaze, if only because I needed to focus on taking stock, but Archie was not phased.

"Nothing," I lied.

"Bullshit. Did something happen yesterday? You've been acting weird ever since the drive home."

I sighed in exasperation once more, figuring resistance was moot.

Besides, I didn't really have anyone else to ask about this sort of thing, so I swallowed my fear.

If I couldn't talk to Archie, who could I talk to?

"Mitchell asked me out."

Archie's eyes widened in surprise. "And you're bothered by that?"

"I said yes." I squealed as I fell back against one of the racks, knocking some boxes loose.

"Oh... I see," Archie said slowly,

nodding. "You're freaking out because you said *yes*."

I stared at the floor, twisting my lips. "I'm freaking out because I don't know how to do this with another guy. I mean, I never considered myself a bad date before, but I don't have the best track record when it comes to relationships."

Archie held my gaze as he locked the stock room door.

"What are you doing?" I asked, panicking.

"Giving us some privacy for the moment," he said seriously.

My blood ran cold at his seriousness.

Archie pulled up a stool, imploring me with his gaze.

"I'm going to ask you something, and I want your one hundred percent honest answer," Archie said, his gaze freezing me in place as much as his tone.

"Okay..."

"Do you like him?" he asked.

It was a simple question that required a simple answer, but somehow it was... complicated.

"I..."

"It's just me, Penn. You can be honest with me."

I thought about his question. About my answer, because I knew the moment I said it out loud, it would be one more break in my glass ceiling.

"I think so."

Archie chuckled. "Pretty sure you wouldn't have said *yes* to a date if you needed persuading."

Something about Archie's tone, his laugh, his ease, made me relax.

I pulled up a stool of my own, my shoulders sinking as I sat down and ran my hands over my face.

"I'm so fucked," I grumbled.

Archie patted me on the back. "Welcome to the club."

His pat turned to a slow rub, that made me sigh.

"What are you so nervous about?"

I sat up straighter, letting my hands fall in my lap as his fell from my shoulders.

"I don't know. Like, historically, I've always been kind of boring on dates in general."

Archie nodded. "So you're worried you'll be a boring date, is that it? Worried you won't make a good impression?"

I shrugged. "Maybe?"

"He asked *you* out, right?" Archie said, crossing his arms.

"Yeah."

"Then I'm pretty sure you have nothing to worry about." Archie said, flashing me with a smile as he got up.

I sighed, hoping he was right.

CHAPTER EIGHTEEN

Penn

I STARED AT myself in my bathroom mirror.

I'd mulled over my appearance, my outfit for the last twenty minutes, and time was dwindling down. Mitchell had offered to pick me up at my house, probably to give us both time to get ready after being in the bakery all day, but I'd spent the last half hour fussing over what to wear and if I could really do this.

It's just a date, you've been on plenty of them.

He asked you *out, you have nothing to worry about.*

Just be cool.

The text on my phone chimed, and I checked it immediately.

Here.

Shit!

He was here!

I let out a deep breath, slicking my hand through my hair one final time, and hoped that things would go smoothly.

It's just hanging out, having dinner.

We did that the other night, while working and everything was fine.

Well, until I ended up kissing him like some swoon-worthy damsel in distress.

But if I was being honest, I *liked* kissing Mitchell.

I wasn't sure if it was him and his suave, smooth air, or if it was just the newness of kissing someone of the same sex, but either way, I couldn't deny that it *did* something for me.

In a way kissing Amy or my exes never did.

Who gets turned on from a *kiss?*

Me, apparently, because just the thought of kissing Mitchell was enough to get me off after I'd gotten home that night.

I pushed the thoughts from my brain, if only because I didn't want to keep my *date* waiting.

I grabbed my wallet, slid it in my pocket along with my cell phone, and was out the door.

"Where are you off to?" my father asked, peering over his newspaper.

I stopped dead in my tracks. I hadn't said anything outright to my parents, mostly because I was still in the *coming home* phase where we hadn't really set boundaries yet, but I was also twenty-three years old. I didn't need my parents' permission to do anything.

But still, it felt weird. Like somehow, some way, they just had parental radar that told them "he's going on a date with a guy!"

I swallowed nervously, turning to face him.

"I'm, uh, just hanging out with Mitchell."

"The photographer?" My dad raised his eyebrow.

I nodded. "Yeah, we're, uh, going to grab a bite to eat. I'll be home late, so don't wait up."

My dad twisted his lips, and I thought he was going to throw a monkey wrench into my evening, call me out or something.

But he only said, "It's nice to see you making friends, Penn. Have fun."

Friends.

Why did that word cut me to the core like a ceramic knife?

I didn't have time to process such things, so I just nodded and headed out the door to see Mitchell leaning against his car, looking absolutely *smokin'*.

His dark hair was gelled back in his usual appearance, and I noted he'd expertly trimmed his facial hair, which made the dark color stand out all the more pronounced against his tanned skin.

He was wearing another one of his flashy shirts, this one bright pink with neon palm trees and aqua inner tubes. Coupled with his black ripped jeans, he looked like Surfer Ken, if Surfer Ken shopped at Hot Topic.

I looked at him, feeling more out of my league than ever.

Especially in my dark wash jeans, my

black converse, and a *nice* pale blue polo.

God, I am such a freaking dork!

I knew I should have worn a button down!

Mitchell's gaze roved over me from head to toe and back again, meeting mine.

"Well, aren't you as pretty as a picture," he said, flashing me a grin as he walked around to open my door.

Instantly, his words caused my blood to rush to my cheeks, but I didn't turn away.

"Thanks," I said with a soft smile, trying to ease my own nerves.

When I was buckled in, and Mitchell had started the car, I realized I was shaking with nerves. I only hoped he couldn't tell.

"So, what did you have in mind tonight?" I asked as he pulled out of the driveway.

"If I told you, I'd have to kill you," he retorted, his voice thick with sarcasm.

I leaned back in the passenger seat, taking a look at his profile.

His pronounced jawline, his sleek, shiny hair.

The fine hair he'd trimmed along said perfect jawline. His skin down over his throat looked so smooth, and I felt an innate desire to run my fingertips along the freshly shaved surface.

God, he was so fucking hot.

Yup, totally out of my league here.

"I think I already died, so what's the difference," I mewled, trying to quiet my twitching cock.

A startling thought coursed through me as I adjusted myself.

What if...

What if Mitchell, like, expects certain things...

I wasn't the type to fuck around on a first date in general; usually, I waited until I at least had some inkling the other person wasn't going to run off immediately.

But just the *thought* of touching someone else's dick made me feel rather conflicted.

The thought of touching *Mitchell's* dick, however...

My cock twitched once again, and I felt a stray sweat break out.

Think unsexy thoughts!

"You okay, Cream Puff?" Mitchell

asked, pulling me from my momentary lapse of sanity.

I crossed my legs, squeezing my cock between my thighs to try and break the spell of desire that had managed to infiltrate my walls.

"Yeah, totally fine. Everything's fine."

Mitchell took a quick side-glance at me.

"You don't have to be nervous, you know. This doesn't *have* to be a date. It can be whatever you want it to be."

I looked at him, thinking about Archie's words.

I swallowed harshly as I nodded.

"I agreed to a date. It's a... date."

Mitchell smiled. "Fair enough."

The rest of the way to our location—which happened to be an outdoor food festival in the city—wasn't as awkward. Then again, when you're listening to the radio and singing carpool karaoke, I suppose it lets off some steam.

I pulled my knees to my chest, wrapping my arms around them as Mitchell disposed of our food.

The park was packed with food trucks lining the streets, but there was ample greenery to sit on and watch the fireworks show Mitchell had mentioned was tonight.

To be honest, I was having a good time. Sharing food, kicking back with a beer, and listening to the bands who were playing was more fun than I thought it would be, and a rather nice surprise.

I'd just set my beer down when Mitchell returned.

The sun had gone down, the sky painted shades of orange sherbet and cotton candy pink with hints of pale blue, and set against its backdrop, Mitchell looked absolutely beautiful.

He was handsome, sure, but his features were dark and stunning.

And I realized at that moment, I didn't just *like* Mitchell DeVille.

I realized I was falling in love with him.

"You ready for some fireworks?" he asked, raising his brow.

I nodded, at a loss for words as the reality hit me. "Uh huh."

His eyebrows furrowed, his arm brushing against mine.

I gazed into his dark eyes and felt like I was treading water in a vast, dark sea.

But I had a feeling that Mitchell would not let me drown.

His gaze dipped to where our arms touched, and I could see he was holding back.

"Are you nervous?" I asked.

Mitchell shrugged. "I told you, you're the one running the show this evening," he said softly.

I chewed my bottom lip.

"I don't want you to hold back because of me," I said, feeling slightly upset that he would even think to do such a thing.

Mitchell's gaze flashed to mine. "I just don't want you to feel like I'm pushing you."

"Because you like me?" It wasn't a question as much as a statement, but when I said the words, I could see the way his entire body relaxed.

"Yeah, Cream Puff. I like you. A lot, actually."

I turned toward him, angling my body closer. I could feel the warmth between us, a cozy fire of our own making.

Archie's words reverberated in my brain. The question I'd been afraid to answer before, wasn't as scary now when I looked at Mitchell.

Instinctively, I reached out, letting my fingertips feel the silkiness of his throat and the freshly shaved skin there. I'd been dying to touch it all evening. The smoothness beneath my fingers was warm and it felt... right.

He felt right.

"I like you, too. A lot," I said, my voice barely a whisper.

I watched as Mitchell closed his eyes, rubbing his cheek against my palm, some of his coarse facial hair scratching my skin.

It wasn't an unpleasant feeling at all, and I found myself wanting to run my fingers over the rough texture lining his jaw.

Wanting to run my fingertips over his lips, into his hair...

I didn't think twice about pulling him to me, about kissing him.

Mitchell groaned in my mouth as my lips moved slowly against his, and I let go just as the first *boom* hit the sky, echoing above us.

When I broke away, I could see the sun had disappeared, dusk taking over and changing the world into something different, something new.

And when I looked in Mitchell's dark eyes, I could see the sparkle like a northern star as the fireworks crackled behind him.

He slid his hand over my neck, his fingers playing with the edges of my hair at the nape of my neck as he pulled me in for another searing kiss.

This...

This is what love is supposed to feel like.

And as we made out underneath the fireworks, I came alive for the very first time.

CHAPTER NINETEEN

Mitch

I PARKED THE car in the parking lot, glancing over at Penn as I contemplated just taking him home. It would have been the gentlemanly thing to do, since I already felt like I was pushing the envelope with him.

But truth was, I liked being around the guy and his golden aura. His sweet disposition, his blushing cheeks. He was fun to mess with, and fun to instigate, and...

He was a really good kisser.

A part of me couldn't believe he'd

agreed to a date in the first place—after all, I knew better than anyone as far as *we* were concerned, this whole *thing* was new for him.

I'd dated my share of men in Jasper Springs, so I understood wholeheartedly the caution of jumping into a relationship with some boy next door like Penn.

But I didn't want to let him go.

Ever.

"Are you okay?" he asked, pulling me from my thoughts.

"What?"

"I mean, we've been parked for five minutes and you, like, zoned out," he said, his eyebrows furrowing together with concern.

"Right, sorry," I said as I looked at him. "You don't *have* to come in, if you don't want to. I can take you home, if you want."

Penn's lips pressed a thin line as he shook his head.

"No, I... want to. Come in. With... you."

"Okay," I said, not wanting to give him a chance to change his mind.

I opened my door and quickly made

my way to open his, my heart in my throat. I knew whatever happened, it could still go south. There was a big difference between making out in the park and making out on my couch.

There was the possibility that he'd get scared and run off, and I'd ruin everything.

"I just want you to know that you're still in charge. We don't have to do anything you don't want to do. We can just watch a movie or something."

I needed him to understand I wasn't pressuring him into anything, and his comfort was my top priority.

Penn nodded as he looked up at me. "I know."

His soft smile tugged at my heart, making it thud so loudly I could hear it in my own ears.

"I just like spending time with you," he admitted.

I nodded, sliding my hand into his. There was no hesitation when he squeezed mine back.

"I think a movie sounds nice."

"All right then," I said as I pulled him down the hall toward my apartment on the bottom floor.

As I stood in front of my door, sucking in a few breaths, I realized just how nervous *I* was.

I opened the door and waved him in, turning on the lights. Once he was in, I closed the door quietly.

"Wow, it's..."

I'd never felt so on the spot before, showing a man my apartment.

Technically, most men didn't make it to see anything past my couch or my bed, so this was new territory for me, too.

"A disaster?" I said, running my hand through my hair as I headed toward the couch, turning on television and queuing up Netflix.

"I was going to say it's pretty chill, actually," he said as he walked around my kitchen, looking like a deer lost in the headlights.

My heart thumped away as I watched him, committing his image in my kitchen to memory.

He looked perfect, standing there, in the light.

I slowly slid my phone out of my pocket and snapped a picture.

"What was that?" he said, startling.

"Nothing, what, uh, what's on your mind? Rom-com, drama? Cartoons?"

Penn chortled at my cartoon comment, and I couldn't help but smile. He was so easy to tease, and I loved it.

My heart echoed as reality hit me like a punch to the gut.

I was falling in love with Penn Baker.

I knew it at that moment as he casually strolled toward me, the golden light of my kitchen lighting him up from behind like an angelic halo.

"Mmm... have you seen Home Again? With Reese Witherspoon?"

I shook my head, dispelling the weird sort of aura that had blanketed me, making me lose my damn mind.

"No, can't say that I have," I said as I sat down, letting the cushions break my fall.

Penn gingerly sat next to me, leaving a modicum of space between us.

I started up the movie.

"Oh, it's a hoot. Reese is a total gem. I used to love Legally Blonde growing up. It was one of my mom's favorites."

I shifted my weight, trying not to appear too desperate, when the truth was all I wanted was to wrap my arm around him, and...

Penn slid across the sliver of space, putting his body flush against mine. I looked down at him, at his perfect, kissable lips, then back to his pretty blue eyes.

"Penn..."

He settled into the open space of my arm, which was stretched along the back of my couch. He shifted his weight, making my body dip toward him, and I was acutely aware of my burgeoning stiffness coming to life.

He leaned in closer, resting his head on my arm as he looked at me with glassy, blue eyes.

"Yeah?" he asked, his eyebrows knitting together with worry.

"Do you have any idea how badly I want to kiss you right now?"

Penn's cheeks flushed and his eyes sparkled with mischief.

"Maybe."

So he wants to play.

I can play.

"I don't think you do."

"Well, what are you waiting for?" he asked, his gaze dipping to my lips.

I hooked my knuckle under his chin,

forcing him to look at me. I needed him to hear my words, really hear them.

His body relaxed under my touch, and my cock twitched with anticipation.

"I want... I *need* to hear you say it," I said, my voice coming out dark and husky. "I need to know what *you* want." I licked my lips. "I need your permission."

"I want..." I watched his pupils dilate, his lips part. Involuntarily, he leaned into me, threading his leg through mine, his hand resting on my knee. He swallowed nervously, but he didn't break my gaze. "I want you to kiss me."

"Is that so?" I asked, hanging on his every word.

He nodded.

So, I kissed him. Softly, my lips caressed his as I let my tongue slip in through the cracks, and he slid his hand around my waist. I could feel the tremble in his touch, but I could also feel the curiosity as he slowly traced his fingers along my hip.

I sucked at his bottom lip as he let out a groan, grabbing me, pulling me closer. I settled my hand on his hip and he leaned into me like a falling star.

His body pressed against mine was

indescribable. My cock twitched as I recognized the similar feeling of his hardness against mine, and I knew I needed to slow down.

But I didn't *want* to slow down. I wanted to make Penn feel as wild and untamed as he made me feel.

I broke apart from him, gazing down at his perfect mouth, lips still swollen from my kiss.

"Is that what you want, Cream Puff?" I asked, tracing my thumb over his bottom lip. "You want to play Netflix & Chill?" I teased.

Penn grinned. "I... I don't know. I just know I want..." His eyebrows furrowed again, as his cheeks flushed.

"Use your words, Penn. I told you, you can be honest with me."

"I just know that I've never felt this... hard from just *kissing* someone."

Well, if that wasn't a boost for my ego, I didn't know what was.

I couldn't help the smile on my face.

His hand on my hip slid down a fraction from our shifted weight, right over my solid erection.

Fuck.

Penn's eyes widened as he yanked his

hand back, like he'd just touched hot iron.

But he didn't move away from me. Instead, his glassy eyes held mine as he let out a shaky breath.

"We can stick to kissing, if you want," I said as I adjusted myself.

Which was when I noticed his legs were pressed together rather tightly, and his face was pink with...

Embarrassment.

Of course, this was all a new sensation for him, and he was probably confused as all hell.

Real smooth, Mitch.

I gently pulled his hand out of his lap, giving it a reassuring squeeze.

"We don't have to—"

"No. I *want* to, I just..."

"Are you sure?" I asked, worried I'd somehow thrown a grenade into an otherwise perfect evening.

Penn nodded. "Usually this is like... third or fourth date material for me. And even then, it's not... I don't feel like... *this.*"

It was my turn to be confused.

"Like what?"

Penn sighed, his cheeks going red.

"Like I'm going to fucking explode in my pants like a damn teenager."

I let out a laugh, because it was funny, but also because as funny as it was, it was also maddening.

"Well, we can't have that," I teased, letting go of his hand.

Penn settled against me once more, curling into me like I was a teddy bear. He reached up, his fingertips trailing over my jaw as he bit his lip.

"And usually there's a discussion about, you know... former partners and all first..."

I watched as he chewed his lip, waiting for my response.

"I can assure you as far as former partners go, I'm clean, Penn. If that's what you're worried about."

His eyes widened as he let out a breath.

"I mean, that's good. Uh... I've only ever been with, like, three people, and uh, I'm good. Nothing to worry about," he said awkwardly.

I brought my lips to his, trying to reassure him this was okay.

Talking about things was normal. Communication was key when it came to relationships, new or old.

He relaxed in my hold, breaking my kiss for only a moment as he let out a breath.

"Good to know," I breathed against his lips.

"Just... go slow, okay?" he said shakily.

I nodded, grasping his hand in mine. "Always," I promised, and he kissed me once more.

I let him lead this time.

Penn's mouth against mine was a torturous sort of desire. He pulled me closer, his hand sliding through my hair and soon, he was beneath me, his breath labored as his kiss transformed into something much more passionate, much more heated than before.

I straddled his hips with my legs, bringing my swollen cock flush against his abdomen. I could feel his erection below me, twitching with interest. I breathed deep as I broke our kiss.

Penn's hands slid over my hip to my front, and he grazed his fingertips over my jean-clad erection.

It was a curious, light touch, and I fought the instinct to grind myself against his palm. I settled against him, my hands on his hips, holding on for dear life.

"Do you like this?" he asked, his voice curious as he looked up at me.

I nodded, kissing him once more. "Yes, Penn. I like making out with you. I like it when you touch me," I said the words plainly, with as much levity as I could.

He needed to know this was okay. That I liked this as much as he did.

That I liked *him*.

Penn swallowed as he held my gaze, *squeezing* my sensitive cock in his hand.

"Fuck," I cursed, trying to hold back.

"Yeah?" he breathed, his breath hot on my skin.

"Fuck, yes," I said, my breath shaky as excitement laced through me.

Penn kissed me once more, letting his thumb rub over the fabric of my jeans where I could feel moisture already pebbling at my slit.

I groaned in defeat as he *thrust* himself against me, whimpering in my mouth with unrelenting truth.

Heat ransacked my body from his explorative touch.

"Tell me what you want, Cream Puff. Tell me and I'll give you *anything* you want." I could hear the desperation in my voice. I'd never begged *anyone* like this before.

The multitude of that was not lost on me, but I felt like I would truly expire if he stopped touching me.

Penn pulled away, letting out a deep breath as he spoke his desires. "I want to see it," he said, his voice dark and full of curiosity.

A smile curved on my lips. "Are you sure?" I asked, grinding myself against his hardness, making my already weeping cock sob all the more.

Penn looked me dead in the eyes, and said, "Yes, I'm sure."

I leaned back on the couch, unfastening my belt and shaking my jeans to the ground along with my boxers. My cock sprang free, precum bathing my tip and glinting in the light. I wrapped my hand around my cock, watching as his gaze dipped to my engorged dick.

Penn sucked in a breath, grabbing himself as he let out his own curse.

"Fucking cherries on top," he

murmured.

"What?" I asked, feeling like maybe I'd gone too far. Maybe this was a terrible idea.

"Archie was so right."

Before I could ask what he meant, Penn *rubbed* himself through his pants, and all senses left me.

Because the sight of him *touching* himself because of me was like a balm to my soul, like a match to my flame.

I stroked myself, noting the way his breath hitched as I did so.

The way his pupils dilated, and his cheeks flushed.

The enormous tent in *his* pants.

I slid my thumb through my precum, coating my pink, swollen head, and Penn groaned in defeat. His gaze practically glued to my cock.

"Like what you see?" I asked, feeling a grin spread on my face.

Penn nodded slowly. "Better than the porn I watched, that's for sure."

I laughed, leaning back as I cocked my head to the side, giving a good thrust into my palm.

Penn cursed under his breath, but he didn't break his gaze.

"Is that what you want, Cream Puff? You want to watch?"

I wanted to go slow because I wanted him to feel comfortable, but I'd be lying if I said I didn't want to explore every inch of Penn's body just to see how he'd react.

Penn's gaze flashed to mine.

"No... I mean, yes. I mean... Fuck, why is this so difficult," he huffed. "Yes. I want to watch you."

I thrust against my palm again, sliding my hand against my shaft.

"But what about you?" he asked, his eyes widening.

"What about me?" I asked, building a slow rhythm as I stroked and pulled my hardness.

"What do you want?"

I grinned wholeheartedly.

"I want whatever you are comfortable with, Penn. I told you, you're running the show."

I half-expected him to just sit there and to continue rubbing himself through his pants, and that would have been just fine for me.

Knowing I turned him on, just with my kiss, seeing his growth as he watched *me* would have been enough to get me off right there.

"Do you like what *you* see?" he asked, his voice taking on a more seductive tone. The curiousness behind it told me he'd likely never tried it before, which gave me another ego boost.

Because he sounded so damn sexy, it was a crime.

Somewhere in the background, the movie droned out and the music played, but it was white noise.

"God, yes, Penn. Can't you see what you do to me? You are killing me," I said as I watched him slide his hand over his giant, jean-clad erection, rubbing himself. "You're the prettiest thing I've ever seen."

Penn slowly slid his hand up and over his covered cock, his head hitting the back of my couch as his eyes closed.

"Fuck," he said, his voice all screwed up. "I don't know if I can do this."

"You're doing such a good job, baby," I said reassuringly, watching as he squeezed his cock, the sound of another whimpering cry escaping his throat.

"Look how well you handle your cock. I bet you'd handle mine just as nice," I purred, stroking myself.

MITCH

The heat, the tension, my own dark and desperate voice mixing with Penn's soft cries was like a firework all on its own.

"Mitch..." he whimpered, his voice all screwed up.

Hearing my name uttered from his lips like that was enough.

I couldn't hold back any longer, my balls tightening and my cock pulsing as the words left me.

"Fuck, I'm coming," my voice strained as I hurried to shift my shirt, giving myself enough of a space to unload on my abs, but I sorely missed, and rope after rope of my cum clung to the satin like Velcro.

I pulled at my buttons, shifting out of my shirt and crumpling it up. Using it to wipe up the last remains of my release, it wasn't until Penn let out a strangled sound that I remembered exactly who I was with, and what had transpired.

I tossed my shirt to the floor, pulling up my jeans as I set my sight on Penn, who looked to be in pain.

I rushed over to him, noting his hand was still squeezing his cock tightly through his pants.

He breathed deeply. His gaze fixed on the ceiling.

"Are you okay?" I asked, concern flooding me.

"I'm so hard it hurts," he muttered.

"Tell me what you need, Penn." I swallowed nervously.

"There's nothing to be embarrassed about here. If you want some privacy or—"

He lifted his head from the couch, his glassy blue eyes full of awe and excitement, and... fear.

"No," he shook his head, his gaze imploring mine.

I ran my hand across his collarbone, letting my fingers find the edges of his hair.

He licked his lips, his entire body relaxing under that one, small touch.

For Penn, this was it.

There was no going back after this.

"I want *you* to make me come."

CHAPTER TWENTY

Penn

I WANT YOU to make me come.

The moment the words left my mouth, I felt lighter, but there was still the overwhelming desire that made it hard to breathe.

I'd never felt for anyone what I felt for Mitchell.

It was truly like I'd been going through the motions, doing what I was *supposed* to be doing, living blindly.

But kissing Mitchell, touching him, feeling his warmth, hearing his *praise*, I knew everything, and everyone before him had been a *lie.*

I'd been living a lie.

In the span of only a few hours, I'd gone on a date, made out with, and watched my hot date blow his load from *watching me.*

If there was any question or any sliver of a chance that I was straight, it had been blown to smithereens now.

Because no one had ever kissed me, flirted with me, or touched me like Mitchell.

No one ever felt this right.

A thousand things came to mind when he asked me what I wanted. I wasn't sure about anything. None of my ex-girlfriends ever really asked what I wanted, and the one night stands didn't really focus on my needs.

I wasn't the type to keep asking either. If my partner didn't want to suck my dick, I wasn't going to push her about it.

My mind was a blur as I tried to process for the first time what it was I wanted, and the decision was as overwhelming as the reality of my throbbing cock pulsing in my hands, the wetness forming at my head, spreading against my boxers.

I just knew I needed to come before I went blind with ecstasy.

"Permission to touch?" Mitch's voice asked, bringing me back down to earth, down to reality.

"Fuck, yes! Please, just make it—"
The *need* to feel his warm palms heating me through my shirt, to feel his fingertips graze over my sensitive skin, was something I'd never experienced with anyone before.

But I wanted more of it. I wanted more of *him.*

The warmth of his hand around mine was like water after a drought.

His hand brushed over my sensitive, strained cock, before gently, swiftly sliding up to unbutton my pants.

Somewhere in my brain, I knew this was it.

Once I let him touch my cock, I knew it would be over.

There was no going back from that.

Almost as if he could sense my turmoil, he spoke.

"If you want me to stop, just say stop, okay?" he breathed, his voice shaking as his hand hovered over my zipper, warming my cock where he had stopped.

My cock *ached* beneath the heat from his palm, separated by metal and denim.

I couldn't help but submit to the desire to thrust myself against his touch, seeking the friction.

Seeking release.

"I don't want you to stop," I breathed, knowing this was my death.

But it was also a sort of rebirth, too.

Because I knew at that moment, I was *his.*

I was completely and utterly at his mercy.

Mitchell held all that I was in the palm of his hand.

I breathed a sigh of relief as he slowly unzipped my pants. Lifting my hips to help him, I let go of the remaining threads of my old self, letting my jeans fall to the ground.

Mitchell gently tugged at the waistband of my underwear, sliding them down just enough to expose me. The minute my cock was free, it was a relief. No more pain as I strained against constricting fabric.

"Fuck," Mitchell cursed, but it wasn't dark and seductive like before.

It was awe-struck.

It was *lovely*.

"You are fucking beautiful," he murmured, the edge of his fingertips brushing against my balls, sliding slowly, achingly slow, against my shaft.

I whimpered in defeat as he closed his hand around my cock.

Mitchell settled next to me, sliding his arm behind me, shifting my body on its side, bringing me closer. I stared at him, shirtless, his dark eyes full of something softer than the lust I felt was consuming me.

His dark hair fell in his eyes, his lips still swollen from kissing me, and he was the sexiest thing I'd ever seen.

And he was slowly, torturously rubbing my cock, and it felt... good.

Better than good, actually.

He kissed me slowly, distracting me from my euphoria for the moment as he slid his tongue in my mouth, and instinctively, I bucked my hips against his hand.

His palm was warm. But his mouth was warmer, and at that moment, I knew exactly what I wanted, and for the first time, I didn't feel awkward, at all. I felt invigorated.

"Mitch," I tried to speak, my linguistics all off-kilter. All I could do was breathe, all my attention pulled to the sensation of his touch as he stroked me, coaxing me closer and closer to the edge as his fingers spread my precum over my shaft like it was freaking lube.

God that feels amazing.

"Yes, baby?" he purred into my mouth, his voice dark, sexy, and absolutely perfect.

He just called me baby.

I think I really might die.

"What does my Cream Puff want, hmm?"

" Please... " I cried. I was so close. I needed to feel his mouth, his tongue on me.

"I like you like this. All needy, and responsive."

A tortured groan escaped me as I thrust myself in his hands, using my own to slide my fingers into his messy, dark hair, to run my fingertips over his rough facial hair, down through the coarse hair on his chest. I let my fingers slide through it, gripping it and committing the touch to memory.

I *liked* how it felt beneath my fingertips.

"Mitch..." I moaned as his mouth accosted mine again. In that kiss, I knew I could do anything.

Mitchell had given me so much already, and I knew all I had to do was ask.

And for the first time in my life, I didn't feel *guilty* about asking for what I wanted. This was it, the final straw, and knowing that made me feel braver, actually.

So, I didn't think twice about what I said next.

"I want you to suck my cock," I breathed, my entire body heating like a flame.

At the reality I'd actually spoken my desires out loud, I added a well placed, "Please."

I didn't want to sound demanding, after all.

Mitchell took my lips again, nipping at my bottom lip as he spread my precum along my already sticky shaft as he slowly pumped me.

"Are you sure, baby?" he murmured, positioning me back on the couch so I was partially laying down, moving his body between my legs.

His fingertips slid up my exposed thighs as my underwear moved down to my knees. I shifted my body, and he gently pulled them down my calves, past my ankles, until they were discarded on the floor, leaving me fully naked from the waist down. I looked down at his face between my thighs, his dark eyes, and hair falling across his temple.

He was stunning, and he was kneeling before me, ready to take whatever I was willing to give.

And something about that realization gave me the courage to reach down, thread my fingers through his hair and push him toward my cock.

Mitchell didn't miss a beat.

He wrapped his lips around my swollen head, and the relief was instant.

His warm mouth felt so fucking good.

He rolled his tongue around my shaft, grazing over my engorged veins, over my slit, and I couldn't help the groan that escaped me.

I watched as he hollowed his cheeks, groaning with his own ecstasy as he built his rhythm. I let out a guttural moan as my hips rocked of their own accord. I gripped his hair with my fingers and I rode his face, shoving my cock down his throat without a second thought. His tongue lapped at my shaft as deep moans escaped him, throwing me over the edge.

It didn't take long at all. Three licks, and he'd found the center of my proverbial tootsie roll pop as I moaned in ecstatic defeat, coming down his throat with a force I'd never felt.

Somewhere in the back of my mind I worried he might not be able to breathe—after all, most of my experience with women had taught me they could only take so much before they literally choked—but such was not the case with Mitchell, who swallowed every drop like my release was nothing more than his favorite drink.

I don't know how long I stayed there, in absolute bliss, but eventually I came back down to earth when I felt Mitchell shift me once more.

"Feel better?" Mitchell asked, his voice tinged with sarcasm.

I curled my half-naked self against him, throwing my arm across his hip as

I *cuddled* him.

He was soft and warm, and safe.

And he made everything feel undeniably *perfect.*

"Mhmmm," I said dreamily.

Perhaps I still was dreaming. I closed my eyes, taking in a deep breath. His facial hair scratched my forehead as his lips pressed a soft kiss to my skin.

"Good. Now get dressed so I can get you home before midnight. I know you need the rest."

"I don't want to go home," I murmured sleepily.

There was a moment of silence, but it wasn't awkward or strange.

It felt comfortable. Because I knew he was there.

"I don't want you to go home either," he whispered. And for the moment that was enough.

The room was silent and I zoned out to the ramblings of the movie and Mitchell's steady heartbeat.

Mine beat in unison with his, and I knew I was a goner.

I was one hundred percent gay for Mitchell DeVille, and I was absolutely head over heels in love with him.

Patient, sarcastic, and sexy as all hell.

I wanted *him*.

"When's your next event?" he asked, pulling me from my swoon-worthy thoughts.

"What?"

"Your next event. So I can photograph it?"

Oh, yeah. That.

I'd almost forgotten Mitchell was technically working for me for the moment.

"Tomorrow night," I yawned. "Engagement party, five o'clock."

"I'll be there."

CHAPTER TWENTY-ONE

Penn

I WALKED INTO the shop and it felt like the sun was shining *everywhere,* despite it being dark and gloomy out. But even as happy as I felt, there was still the nagging bit of my psyche that was still coming to terms with just how far Mitchell and I had gone on our date.

Usually, I preferred to keep things PG until the third or fourth date, partially out of respect, but also because, prior to Mitchell, it took a while for me to build up the desire to *want* to be intimate with my partners.

Which probably should have been my first clue.

And there I was, on my first date with a dude, with my dick down his throat by the end of the night.

Did that make me a slut?

Archie came in at that exact moment as my existential crisis hit.

"I'm doing a half day today, leaving around ten."

"What?" I said, blinking, trying to dispel my thoughts.

"I told you yesterday, it's my cousin's birthday."

"Right," I said, trying to remember.

Archie came over to me, approaching me like a wary animal.

"Yikes? Was it that bad?" he asked, his eyebrows furrowing with concern, his words pulling me from my thoughts.

"What?"

"You're grimacing. Either it's a cake disaster or your date tanked."

"My date... Yeah, uh, about that..."

Archie grabbed an apron, tying it around his waist as I ran my hands over my face.

"What happened?"

"Things, uh, might've gotten a little

hot and heavy last night." I chewed my lips, avoiding his gaze.

Archie yelped with excitement. "Yes! That's awesome! It is awesome, right? Or did it suck?"

His choice of words made my cheeks flush with heat, and before I could say anything, he slapped me on the back.

"They grow up so fast," he said approvingly.

"No, it didn't suck. It was probably the best blowjob I've ever had, to be honest."

Archie smirked. "Of course it was. So what's the problem then? Why the long face?"

I let out a deep breath as I grabbed the rag and cleaner to polish up the counter.

"I mean, I've never done anything like that on a first date before," I admitted.

Archie picked up what I was throwing down.

"Ahh, I see. So you think he's going to think you're easy, is that it?"

I bit my lip, my jaw tensing. "I mean, I don't want him to think that's all I'm about, or what I'm after, you know?"

Archie sighed. "Did you feel

pressured?"

"No," I said, turning around, shaking my head. "Not at all."

"Who made the move?" Archie asked. My cheeks heated once more.

"What do you mean?"

"Did he offer? Or did you ask?"

My cock twitched at the memory of the words leaving my mouth, of the memory of his warm tongue wrapped around my aching cock.

"I asked," I whispered, even though at this hour there was no one here but us.

Mitchell was meeting me after work for the event, and my parents were only doing the orders today, so they'd be in and out by noon. Which meant, for the majority of the day, I'd be here by myself, prepping cupcakes for tonight's event.

"And you asked because *you wanted it*, right? Not because you thought you had to?" Archie pressed.

"Well, yeah, I mean, it just felt right at the time, I guess."

Archie smiled softly. "If it feels right, it's right, Penn. No matter who it is, or when it happens."

Something about his words settled

something inside of me, and I sighed.

"I guess that makes sense."

Archie nodded. "Don't over think everything. You'll drive yourself crazy. Just do what feels right. Listen to your heart and shit."

I shook my head, a light laugh escaping me. "Is that what you do? Listen to your heart?" I teased.

Archie smirked. "I listen to my dick, but one day when my heart speaks up, I'll know."

"How do you know I'm not listening to my dick?" I taunted him.

"Oh, I know you're listening to your dick," he drawled, both of us laughing. "But I also know that you're not the type to casually get intimate either. Your heart pumps blood to your brain and your dick. They all work together you know."

"I know. I was the one who actually passed Biology, remember?" I said as I went about my cleaning.

"All I'm saying, is you don't do anything half-assed. Give yourself a little more credit, Penn. Trust yourself."

I nodded in understanding. Archie was right. I did need to give myself more credit. I knew my worth, and I had a feeling Mitchell knew it, too.

CHAPTER TWENTY-TWO

Mitch

I KNEW WE didn't have to be at the event until four thirty, but I couldn't stop thinking about Penn, and what had happened between us.

It seemed wild to me that I'd barely known the guy a little more than a week, and somehow, some way, I'd become a total simp for the man.

I wasn't usually the type to get attached so quickly, and while I loved where things were going with us, I was also scared of how quickly Penn had stolen my heart.

Because the truth of the matter was, I loved the guy.

I loved the sparkle in his pretty blue eyes, the way he blushed, the way he *teased* me, the kindness of his heart, the gentleness of his soul.

And I really, really loved kissing him.

I loved the way he brought out a side of me that no one else had ever been able to access.

Which is probably why I'd convinced myself to show up early to the shop.

Penn looked up from behind the counter as the door jingled.

"Hey," he said, surprised.

"Afternoon," I said, sauntering in with just my camera bag. Today, I wanted to shoot Penn in his element freehand, capture a more candid feel for this set of images.

And after combing over wedding photos all morning, I couldn't deny Penn in his little white, cake-stained apron, blond hair shimmering in the light, was like a breath of fresh air.

My own personal Cream Puff.

"I thought we were meeting up at the event," he said, and he turned to the back counter, which I could see was covered in cupcake trays, not all of them full.

With his back turned to me, I quietly brought out my camera, zooming in on the lineup.

"I thought I'd come in and get some solo shots of you," I said, clicking away.

Penn headed to the bowl of batter on the steel table in the corner, grabbing a large bowl and scoop.

Click.

"Where's Archie at?"

Penn shrugged, letting out a sigh as I went behind the counter, tucking myself into a corner as I watched him.

"Uh, he had a thing, I guess. Took a half day."

I framed the trays as I watched him scoop some batter into the first tray.

"And your parents?"

Penn chortled. "They've got a more active social life now that I'm home, working. They left this afternoon to go stay with some friends for the weekend in the city."

"So, it's just you running the ship today? And you have an event?"

Penn sighed once more. "Yeah, I guess it looks that way."

"You've been working every day this week. Don't you get a day off?"

Penn shrugged. "I mean, I've been gone for months, so I'm making up for lost time, I guess."

"Still, you're human. Humans need rest."

Penn hurriedly set his bowl down, turning around and looking for something, a confused look on his face.

I set my camera down. "Looking for something?"

"Uh, yeah, the cupcake liners. They're...."

I noticed them out of the corner of my eye, behind my camera. I picked them up, heading over to Penn, who reached for them. I pulled them out of his reach.

"Mitch, come on..."

"You scoop, I'll line."

Penn pursed his lips. "You don't have to—"

"Maybe I want to."

I watched as his eyebrows furrowed, and his shoulders relaxed.

"I'm not used to help. I mean, Archie has his own duties, and my parents, well, when they're here everything is pretty much done already, and I—"

I hip-checked him, nudging him toward his bowl as I started to peel the liners out of the stack, placing them in each muffin cup in their prospective trays.

"You've already helped me so much, it feels like I'm taking advantage. I wish there was something I could do to show my thanks," he said softly, taking the hint and grabbing his bowl of batter, following behind my lining.

I chuckled darkly. "I could definitely think of a few ways you could show your gratitude," I teased.

Like I expected, Penn's cheeks blushed with that perfect pink tint.

"Mitch!" he squealed, but it wasn't angry or worried. It was tinged with laughter, and only a hint of embarrassment.

"What? I told you when we first met, I like sugar. And cream."

Penn shook his head as he moved down the line to fill more of the lined cups as I added, "And you *did* promise me sweet, sugary goodness."

I turned toward him as I reached the end of the line. Penn grasped the bowl tightly as he glanced up at me, rosy cheeks and glassy eyes making my damn cock twitch and my heart beat faster.

"Would dinner suffice?" he asked, raising an eyebrow.

His bowl of batter was practically empty, and I couldn't help myself. I ran my finger along the inside of the rim, collected a small amount of the creamy goodness on the tip, and took a lick of the batter.

Penn licked his lips, tightening his grip on the bowl.

"You know there is raw egg in that?" he warned.

I licked the batter off my finger with a moan of delight.

Vanilla cream.

Fucking delicious.

"Yeah, and it's delicious."

"Help me put these in the ovens," he said, averting his gaze as he picked up the first tray with one hand, popping open the top and bottom oven doors.

I gladly grabbed two trays and followed suit, loading them in.

Penn grabbed the last tray and put it on the bottom rack, closing the doors.

"To answer your question, where did

you have in mind? For dinner, I mean.”

Penn cleaned up his dishes, setting out new things. A piping bag, a bucket of frosting.

I glanced at the label, to see the frosting was also vanilla.

I picked up my camera once more, watching as he separated the vanilla frosting into two separate bowls, coloring the one with red food coloring.

Snap! Click!

“I was thinking maybe since, uh, my parents are out of town, you could, you know, come over to my place and I could *make* dinner? Unless of course, you’d rather go somewhere, or—”

My heart skipped a beat as I realized he was asking me over to his place.

On his terms.

And he wanted to make me dinner.

The excitement coursing through me was unimaginable.

I never said yes so fast in all my life.

Granted, I knew I still had lots of work to do on both his images and the wedding, but there was nothing I wanted to do more than spend time with Penn Baker.

“I’d like that,” I said as the oven timer

went off.

Penn tossed me some oven mitts, hitting me square in the chest.

"So bossy," I said as I set my camera down, dressing my hands with the bright blue oven mitts.

Within seconds, Penn had the first two trays, and I had the rest, setting them down on the steel table in the center of the kitchen.

They smelled heavenly.

Once set, Penn pulled his mitts off and I did the same, following him as he loaded up his icing into piping bags.

"You said you wanted to help..."

I smiled at his *whine*. I swore there wasn't anything I wouldn't do for my little Cream Puff, if he asked so nicely.

Hell, who was I kidding?

I'd do anything for him if he looked at me with those pretty blue eyes and those perfect, kissable lips.

Penn tied off the end, and handed one to me.

"I'll do these two, you do those two, okay?" he said, nodding to the trays in front of me.

"Yes, boss," I teased him, watching the smile form on his face from my words.

I watched Penn out of the corner of my eye, his focus on his cupcakes stern.

Unbreakable almost, which gave me an idea.

"Hey, Penn," I called his attention and he looked up, and I squeezed a dab of icing right on his cute little nose.

"Gotcha," I said with a grin.

Penn huffed as he swiped the frosting off his face. "Asshole," he teased, but his voice was full and light.

"You just looked so serious," I said, heading back to my cupcakes.

"I was concentrating," he defended.

"Uh huh," I said as I focused back on my last tray.

"Hey, Mitch..." he called, nonchalantly.

"Yeah?" I looked up, and was met with a *smattering* of icing across my face as his fingertips slid across my cheek.

"You little..." I cursed as Penn jumped back, holding up his bag of frosting like a sword.

"Not so funny when you're the target, is it?" he teased.

I grabbed my own bag in defense. "I'm going to get you for that."

Penn's smile was infectious, his pristine blue eyes sparkling like diamonds in the afternoon light.

"I'd like to see you try," he said, giggling as he took off, and I chased after him.

We ran through the bakery, spraying pink and white vanilla frosting at one another in retaliation, and the sounds of our combined laughter filled the air.

Penn hurriedly flipped the sign from open to closed, all while dodging me as I tried to catch him like a wild gingerbread man.

When I finally did catch him, it was just as he was coming around the front counter, and I grabbed him by his apron ties, pulling him backward and into my arms.

We were both covered in frosting, panting from our chase. The light from the windows behind him lit him up, showcasing the stark white cream all over his cheeks, his neck.

His lips.

I didn't think twice about pressing him against the wall and licking the sweet cream off of his gorgeous face. As I did so, I could feel his cock hard against my own, and he wrapped his arms around me, the tip of his piping bag poking me in the back as he held it.

I licked the frosting from his lips, biting gently at his bottom one.

The throaty moan that left his throat went straight to my cock.

Penn kissed me back, melting into me once more, before he squeezed himself out from under me, heading back to the last tray of cupcakes.

I didn't miss the smile on his face as he finished decorating, or the words that were caught in my throat.

Those three little words I'd almost said out loud.

"We've got less than an hour to finish these and get to the party," he said, pulling my attention once more.

"Right," I said, shaking my head.

CHAPTER TWENTY-THREE

Penn

I COULDN'T EXPLAIN it, but it was like ever since the night before, when we'd gone on our date, when I let Mitchell touch me, when I asked him to suck my damn dick, it was like a switch had been flipped.

I couldn't stop thinking about him. About his talent, about his smirk, about his sexy voice. About how he was always giving *me* the reins to control where we were going.

Because deep underneath all the vibrant shirts and sarcasm, Mitchell *cared* about my needs, my comfort.

After my conversation with Archie, I thought a lot about what he said. About things just feeling right.

About how I'd *asked* for Mitchell to bring me my release.

About how my fingers gripping his hair while he did so and how it was the purest ecstasy I'd ever felt.

And I guess you could say I was curious if I was capable of providing Mitchell with the same amount of pleasure he gave me.

I tossed my chicken in the pan, feeling Mitchell's gaze on my backside, and the instinct to blush took over once more.

Even though I couldn't see him, I could feel his appreciation, how he studied me.

Plus, I could hear the faint sound of a shutter clicking every few moments.

"You really didn't have to do this, you know," he said.

I gave the chicken another toss as the pasta continued to boil on the stove. I turned to look at him, sitting there at the counter and the nerves came rushing back.

MITCH

Could I do this?

Was I absolutely, certifiably insane?

Most of my relationships, the serious ones anyway, didn't last long. I was with Amy for all of eight months, and that was my longest relationship.

I'd made dinner for her a few times, but it was still awkward after.

Sex with Amy wasn't *bad*, but it wasn't anywhere near the amount of rapture I experienced with Mitchell.

I looked at him sitting there in my kitchen, and my heart skipped a beat.

"The way to a man's heart is through his stomach," I said, flashing him with a nervous grin.

I had this grand idea that we'd have dinner, then maybe we could make dessert, together, and then...

My cheeks flushed with heat as the thought I'd been keeping at bay all day crept into my brain.

I swallowed harshly, turning away from Mitchell to avoid giving away my embarrassment at my wayward thoughts.

"Well, you had me hook line and sinker with those cream puffs. And the cinnamon rolls."

I turned off the burner for the pasta, drained it and moved about my kitchen with precision.

"I mean, those were part of the agreement. This..."

I realized within seconds Mitchell was behind me. Setting his hand just above my ass.

He leaned in closer, his lips close to my ear. "Is not part of the agreement, I know," he murmured, his breath hot on my neck.

I quickly added the pasta to the oversized skillet with the chicken and cream sauce, then I turned to look at him. His dark hair fell in his eyes seductively, and all the nerves that had been making my stomach flip all day dissipated.

I was without a doubt, in love with Mitchell DeVille.

The world around me fell away when he looked at *me.*

When he touched me.

When he kissed me.

"No, it wasn't," I breathed, my gaze dipping to his lips. I didn't think twice about pressing my lips to his.

As far as I was concerned, I could

kiss Mitchell forever and ever.

I could feel his grin at the corner of his mouth as he slipped his tongue between my parted lips.

My entire body eased from his touch and I let my hand rest on his hip for a brief moment.

A soft laugh erupted from my throat as I reluctantly pulled away from him, and fumbled for the knob to turn off the skillet.

Looking back at him over my shoulder as he pressed himself up behind me, I knew this was it for me.

I'd looked and looked for the right person, but I had been looking in the wrong places.

There was a reason my previous relationships hadn't been successful.

Because they were one-sided, and they weren't *him*.

I wasn't sure how to define myself just yet, but I knew without a doubt I was one hundred percent gay for Mitchell.

Probably only *Mitchell*.

I broke away, my entire body warm as a grin spread over my face.

"You are so distracting, you know

that?" I teased.

Mitchell hummed lowly, the sound dark and inviting and going straight to my cock.

Which did not help matters as the fantasy I'd been brushing off all day came back full force.

"I like distracting you. You get all flustered, and it's fucking adorable," he purred, his voice gruff and filled with a seductive tone.

I rolled my eyes as I gingerly pushed against his chest. "Sit down, please. I need to plate *your* dinner."

Mitchell tugged my hips closer, putting me right against his rigid erection. "Penn..."

"Dinner first," I said kissing him chastely. "Then dessert."

Mitchell sighed, but relented, and I hated the feeling when he removed his palm from my waist.

CHAPTER TWENTY-FOUR

Penn

"OH MY GOD, is there anything you don't do?" Mitchell groaned as he made his way through his second bowl of pasta.

I shrugged, twisting the noodles around my fork. "Well, there are a couple things..." I said nonchalantly.

I was still nervous because as the night drew on, we were getting closer and closer to my big plan.

Would I chicken out?

Would I get up close and personal with Mitchell's cock and run the other way?

Or would I be able to stomach it in my mouth?

What if I was *terrible* at sucking dick?

Worse?

What if I couldn't take it?

"I really appreciate your helping out with the campaign and all," I said, shifting the conversation to one that wasn't going to give me a heart attack.

I took a bite of my pasta, finishing my plate.

Mitchell got up and brought his dish to the sink, and I followed suit.

"I'm glad to do it, you know. It's definitely something different for me. Usually, I'm stuck photographing weddings and engagements, and corporate events. This is a nice change, something I can add to my portfolio," he said.

I nodded for him to follow me to the living room. Our house wasn't huge by any means, but before my mom had the shop, my dad had blown out the original wall separating the kitchen and living room and turned it into an open concept, which helped in those days because mom was always baking up a storm. A few card tables and TV trays in conjunction with the counters was basically her operating bakery.

"You don't like shooting weddings or engagements?" I asked as we took a seat on the couch. Mitchell settled in easily as I reached for the remote, fully intending to actually *watch* a movie while our food settled and then we could make dessert.

I'd planned for something simple; a peach crisp, topped with some vanilla bean ice cream.

But we wouldn't get that far.

"I don't dislike it, but..." Mitchell sighed, looking away from me. His voice softened. "A lot of the time I can just focus on the job, but sometimes... sometimes it just hits different, you know?"

I did know.

My heart sank as I watched his jaw tense, his body sinking into my couch.

I knew exactly what it felt like sometimes to watch two people, so in love, celebrate their bright future together when you were single.

When all you wanted was someone who would look at you the way they looked at each other.

I reached for him, pulling him toward me to settle my arm around him, like he had with me.

Looking into his eyes, I was overwhelmed with emotion and fantasy, with love and anxiety.

"I know exactly what you mean, Mitch," I said, hoping he could understand.

How could I make him understand what I barely comprehended myself?

"Penn…"

I leaned in, capturing his lips with mine.

Mitchell melted against me, a deep satisfying groan leaving his throat.

I slid my hands down the expanse of his chest, feeling the solidness through the fabric of his banana print silk shirt. The image of him shirtless before me replayed in my brain and I slid my hand beneath the hem of his shirt. I trailed my fingers over his warm skin, against the waistband of his jeans.

His hand found mine as he gently pushed me away.

"Penn…" he whispered my name, and I couldn't deny I liked the way it sounded.

I took his bottom lip into my mouth as I grabbed his hip, pulling him closer, my cock straining against my jeans once more.

Fuck dessert.

Mitchell is all I want.

Mitchell's body loosened as I leaned forward, backing him up against the armrest, settling my body between his legs, his hardness pressing against me causing an influx of heat to my entire body.

Mitchell pushed me away, breaking our kiss. "Penn, hold on."

Panic and anxiety flooded me.

Had I done something wrong?

Had he changed his mind about me?

About us?

I looked up at him, his lips still swollen from kissing me, his dark eyes glassy.

"What's wrong?" I asked, realizing that perhaps this *wasn't* about me.

I sat up straighter, reaching for his hand. I hated to see anything but excitement and mischief in those eyes.

"I just... You don't *need* to do this, you know," he said, swallowing hard. "I don't want you to feel like you *have* to because of..."

I shook my head.

This again.

"When are you going to realize that I *want* this? I want *you*," I said.

The sigh of relief that left him was indescribable.

I slid my fingers in between his, squeezing as I continued. "I get that you're trying to give me space to figure things out, and I appreciate that more than you know. But you..."

I swallowed nervously as the words made their way out of my throat. "You feel right. This... feels right. Doesn't it?" I asked, afraid of his answer.

Because, with one word, Mitchell DeVille could bring it all to a halt.

And that terrified me more than anything else. Because I didn't want my time with him to end when this job did.

He'd wedged himself into my heart and my life, and I didn't want to go back to the way things were before I met him.

When I was just existing. Without knowing who I was.

Without knowing him.

Without knowing what *right* felt like.

And when the words left me, they were the truest ones I'd ever said.

"When it's right, it's right. No matter who it is."

CHAPTER TWENTY-FIVE

Mitch

SOMETHING SETTLED IN my heart the moment Penn said those words. He felt like I was *right*.

That this connection, this fire between us, was right. That despite how it happened, it had happened, and the only one preventing us from moving forward was me.

Because I was scared he'd burn through me and leave me in a pile of ash to seek out better dick because that's what everyone else did.

I was scared that he'd wake up one

day and realize this was just some experiment, and not anything *real.*

But as I looked at Penn Baker's pretty blue eyes, I knew.

This was more than just real.

This was *it.*

Penn was everything I'd ever wanted, and everything I thought I could never have.

I leaned into him without thinking, crashing my lips to his. His smooth, plush lips slowly moved against my own as I slid my fingers into the edges of his hair, and he slid his hands down my side, moving one to settle over my straining cock. His hand stayed there for a moment, rubbing and teasing me over my jeans.

I couldn't help the moan that escaped my mouth as my cock twitched, automatically pressing up toward the heat of his hand.

Penn slid his tongue in my mouth as he settled between my legs once more, his lips finding their way to the corner of my mouth, along my jaw, my neck.

H explored me with his lips as he shifted my body beneath him, backing me up against the arm of the sofa.

I closed my eyes in ecstasy as his lips trailed over my skin, one hand pulling at my collar while the other slowly unbuttoned my jeans.

I wanted to protest. To throw up my walls of protection and give him the out.

He must have felt my hesitation, because he whispered into my car, "Tell me to stop and I'll stop."

I shook my head, burying my lips in his hair, at the shell of his ear.

"I don't want you to stop, Cream Puff."

Penn yanked on my zipper, and I grunted as he fumbled with my jeans, shifting us both as I arched my hips off the cushion to give him better access. His hands did not shake, and there was no tremble in his voice, in his kiss, or his touch.

Penn ran his warm palm over my sheathed cock, gabbing mc through my boxers, squeezing me.

Fucking hell.

"Penn..." I groaned.

"Yeah?" he whispered, his thumb separating the thin opening.

"I—"

My words died on my tongue as he

pulled my cock through the opening of my boxers, the cool air kissing my shaft like a balm.

He wrapped his hand around me, slowly stroking me into muteness.

I couldn't speak, nor could I process anything except his slow, curious touch.

He settled himself between my legs, using one hand to cup my balls while the other slowly stroked me. I could feel the moisture pebbling at my head. I expected him to continue with this new exploration, touching, rubbing, maybe even grinding, but...

The last thing I expected was to feel a hot, wet mouth wrap around my cock.

"Fuck!" I cried out as my cock hit the back of his throat.

I grit the curse through my teeth as the wind was knocked out of me.

Within seconds, Penn was off of me, leaving my cock wet, throbbing, and aching for *more*.

"Are you okay? Did I hurt you?" he asked, his eyebrows furrowing with concern.

A laugh erupted from my chest.

"No, you didn't hurt me. Just took me by surprise is all," I said, looking at his swollen lips, his bright eyes focused on me.

His lips were so close to my cock. I bucked my hips, brushing my wet tip against his lips and he smirked. I wondered if this breath of fresh air would deter him, but it didn't.

I watched as his tongue darted out to lick the drop of precum off my tip, and he didn't gag or convulse or even make a disgusted face.

He grabbed me by the base with one hand, his other still cupping and massaging my balls as he swallowed and dived back in.

"Fuck, I was right. You take my cock so fucking well." I groaned.

A contented sound escaped his throat as he massaged my balls, using his other hand to stroke me while he licked and sucked, groaning with his own euphoria.

"Your mouth feels so good." I moaned, letting my fingers find the back of his head as I gently guided him forward to take more of me.

Penn picked up my request, once again, taking me to the back of his throat without warning.

"Fucking hell, Penn... I'm going to—"

Penn hollowed his cheeks, sucking, licking, and groaning around my cock like I was his favorite dessert, and I couldn't contain myself.

My back arched off the cushions as my balls tightened, my spine tingled, and the onslaught of my orgasm ricocheted through me. My cock pulsed as I came, hard and fast.

I half expected Penn to jump back at the first taste, but he only gripped me tighter.

Swallowing every bit of my release down his throat like my cock was a damn keg at a frat party.

And when I was done, he released me, leaning back on his heels as he *wiped* some of the remains of my cum from his swollen, perfect lips, and I couldn't contain myself.

I lunged forward, tearing his pants off.

Penn's cock sprang forth, bobbing in the air. His head was slick with precum, his veins thick and pronounced.

"Did you like that, my little Cream Puff?" I purred, Penn's eyes widening at my gruff tone, his golden hair all disheveled, sticking out from the static of the couch cushions that cradled his head.

He licked his pouty lips, his gaze heated and dark with lust.

It was like something flipped inside of me the minute he said those three words.

I want you.

Like the veil had been lifted, and suddenly, we were both in uncharted territory.

Penn grabbed himself, his gaze fixed on mine as he nodded. "Yes," he said the word firmly. It was not a whisper.

It was an admission.

I grabbed his hand, pulling it away as I settled on my elbows between his legs.

His voice softened for a moment as he leaned himself up on his elbows, looking down at me with curiosity and asked, "I did good, right?"

I nodded my head, a dark chuckle leaving my throat.

"So good, baby," I praised, licking him from shaft to head, watching him shiver with excitement. "Like you were made to suck *my cock.*"

I watched his cheeks tint that

wondrous shade of pink, watched him bite his lip at my praise.

"God, you are so fucking beautiful, you know that, right?" I said, staring at him for a moment, taking in the sight of him before me like this.

Messy blond hair, bright blue eyes, and a thick, gleaming cock bouncing free, just waiting to be devoured.

A perfect specimen waiting to be worshipped.

I ran my tongue up his shaft, taking pleasure in the way Penn squirmed under my attention, and I couldn't deny I loved him like that.

Desperate.

Needy.

He thrust his cock at me, hips bucking of their own accord, and I grabbed him by the base. I ran my tongue over his leaking head and he cursed.

"Mitch..." he begged.

I nipped and sucked at his head, groaning in response. "Yes, Cream Puff?"

"Please...." he begged, his voice getting all screwed up again.

A salacious smile curved on my lips.

God, I loved this man.

"Please, what?" I taunted as I settled one hand underneath his ass cheek, digging my fingernails in as I pulled my attention away from his cock for a moment to watch the look on his face. His dilated pupils met my gaze, and in his eyes I could see the need, the trust.

"Please make me come," he voiced his words with boldness, with confidence this time, and I couldn't help but smile.

I would give this man anything he asked for.

"You are so pretty when you beg," I praised.

Penn whimpered in defeat, his chest heaving with breath.

"Fucking hell." His head fell back. "You are killing me..."

"How could I tell you no?" I murmured, and I took his cock in my mouth, lavishing his thickness with my tongue as I squeezed his ass.

"Oh my God... Mitch... I—" Penn's legs squeezed the sides of my face as his voice strained.

He was so close.

So fucking close.

"God, I fucking love you," I murmured the words without thinking.

Fuck!

"Wh... what?" he asked, nearly breathless.

It wasn't untrue, I did love him, but the last thing I wanted to do was push him away with such an admittance. Nothing *killed* the mood quite like an unrequited admission of love in my experience.

So instead, I did the only thing I could think of to distract us both from said admission.

I took Penn into the back of my throat, groaning my appreciation around his cock, my tongue sliding over his thick veins, and brought him the release he begged for. The pleasure he more than deserved.

"Oh my God," he mewled, thrusting his cock in my mouth as he emptied himself, hot and creamy, down my throat.

When his body went limp, I let go, and reality blanketed us once more. I settled back on my heels as I watched his chest heave with his breaths, watched his pupils slowly return to normal.

Ecstasy had been replaced with

anxiety as his eyebrows furrowed, and he looked me over.

I'd fucked up.

Shit.

"Mitch..." he breathed through labored breaths.

I grabbed my pants, pulling them back up around my legs as I stood, collecting the shards of myself I'd just laid bare for Penn to see.

Fuck.

I need to get out of here before disaster hits.

Before I break apart at the seams.

"I'm sorry," I said as I zipped my zipper, buttoning my pants. "I should go..."

Penn stood, dressing himself. There was only a modicum of space between us, but it felt like a canyon.

I needed air.

I needed to preserve what dignity I had left, because surely I'd just ruined everything.

"Mitch..." his voice softened, and I hated it. The sadness, the disappointment.

I grabbed him, kissing him with all that I was, hoping he could feel my truth. Hoping it would be enough to make him forget my words, no matter how true they were.

"I'm sorry, Penn," I said. "I'll see you tomorrow afternoon."

CHAPTER TWENTY-SIX

Penn

I WATCHED HIM leave and I just stood there.

Frozen, like an ice cube.

Mitchell said he loved me.

Granted, it was with my cock down his throat, but the admission itself struck me in the chest like Cupid's arrow.

Time moved slowly and all at once as I tried to grasp onto those words, tried to keep them alive and in the air.

God, I fucking love you.

I'd never told anyone I loved them.

But at that moment, I wanted to say *yes*. Yes, I love you, too.

But then I was distracted by Mitchell's expert tongue and my impending orgasm, and the world around me disappeared.

Once again, I was at the mercy of Mitchell DeVille, and there was nothing I could do except ride out the bliss until I'd fallen back to earth.

I reached for him. I needed to touch him, to know he was real. I needed to tell him how I felt, but I was scared.

Everything was just happening so fast.

I could barely keep up with my own emotions, let alone the ones Mitchell had obviously buried.

I wanted to soothe him, to tell him it was okay.

I loved him, too.

But the world around me slowed to a crawl as he dressed himself, kissed me, and left.

And I just let him.

Because I was afraid of chasing after him.

I was afraid he was running *away from me.*

I absentmindedly colorized my five bowls of frosting, numb to the world around me. I barely heard Archie when he spoke.

"What is with you today? Earth to Penn?" he said, waving a spatula in my face.

"This wouldn't have anything to do with that photographer boy would it?" my mom's voice cut through, bursting my bubble, as Archie screeched, "What?"

My Mom set down the tray of sugar cookies, which I needed to ice for the Pride Fundraiser we were working tonight.

She did not look at all phased.

"I mean, you two have been attached at the hip lately in a... non-friendly way."

My cheeks heated immediately. "Mom!"

Archie laughed, but my mother only crossed her arms as I loaded the piping bags.

"What? A mother *knows* when her son is in love."

I wasn't sure how to proceed with her insinuation, but figured honesty was the best policy.

Even if it was uncomfortable.

"Yeah, well, it's a bit more complicated than that."

My mother grabbed the red piping bag to start working on a tray.

It reminded me of Mitchell, who'd just shoved his way into helping me just the other day, and I felt sick all over again.

What if I'd fucked up because I didn't say anything?

Because I didn't go after him?

What if he never wanted to see me again?

"Anything worthwhile isn't easy."

"Your mom is right. Whatever happened, I'm sure it can be fixed," Archie said.

I chewed my lips as I lined the cookies my mom passed down to me with blue lines.

"I just... should have told him the truth. But I didn't."

My mom settled her arm around me. "So tell him now. There's no expiry on telling someone how you feel."

I glanced up at her, feeling my heart catch in my throat as she rubbed my shoulders like she used to do when I was afraid. When I was a kid.

My voice shook as I fell apart under

my mom's gaze.

"Even if it's a guy?"

My mom pulled me in close, wrapping me in a tight embrace and I hugged her, my shoulders loosening and my head buried in her apron.

"Baby, I wouldn't care if he was an alien from Mars. As long as he makes *you* happy, that's all that matters."

I could feel Archie's hand on my back as he softly spoke, too. "When it's right, it's right, no matter who it's with."

Something inside me clicked, knowing that I had their support. That I wasn't doing this alone, and as scary as it was, I had back up.

I had people who understood me and supported me.

And that included Mitchell.

The man I loved.

"Thanks, Mom," I said as she broke our hug to return to her piping.

"You don't have to thank me, sweetheart," she said, and with that I knew exactly what I needed to do.

CHAPTER TWENTY-SEVEN

Mitch

I WASN'T THE biggest fan of the Jasper Springs Pizza, but I was feeling like a damn asshole, and I guess the cheese blanketed the guilt enough.

"What's your deal today? You look like someone stole the last cookie from the cookie jar," Dawson nipped.

Cade sipped his drink before chiming in. "Dawson's right. You seem more sullen than usual. Does this have anything to do with that guy from karaoke? Pete, was it?"

"Penn," I said his name, feeling it

echo in every part of my being.

Nolan tapped away on his phone, but I didn't miss his glance.

I sighed, picking at my crust.

"I mean, kind of, yeah."

"Do you want to talk about it?" Weston asked cautiously.

I sighed, knowing it was best to just get it over with. Maybe then they'd let me eat my feelings in peace.

"He's new. To, you know, guys."

"Ah," Dawson said. "So you're worried he doesn't really like *you*."

Penn had told me he did, but I guess old habits died hard.

"And you really like him," Cade chimed.

I didn't even have to answer them. Instead, I just groaned in defeat.

"Yeah, and on top of all of that, I said I love you. By accident."

Dawson smirked. "So you really like him, then."

"Yes, Dawson. I fucking love him okay, are you happy? Is that what you want me to say?" I snapped.

Cade sighed. "He didn't say it back, obviously."

I huffed in annoyance. "Obviously.

But that's probably because his dick was down my throat."

Nolan laughed.

"What's so funny Pencil-Pusher?"

Nolan set his phone down. "Nothing."

"So let me get this straight, you're worried you fucked shit up because you were *honest* about your feelings?" Weston asked seriously.

Well, when he put it that way...

"I mean, I don't even know *what* I am to him, but—"

"What is he to you?" Cade asked.

Everything.

My lack of response was probably telling enough.

"How did this become so fucking complicated?" I asked, running a hand over my face.

Dawson piped in, his tone serious. "Don't tell me to fuck off, but I want your honest answer."

I shot him a glare, and he continued.

"Did you give him a *chance* to talk about it?"

Dawson giving me relationship advice was the equivalent of hell freezing over. The man was notorious for his lack of commitment.

At least, he was until he met Nolan.

I'd replayed the moment over and over in my mind, but suddenly I saw it with startling clarity.

I'd *avoided* Penn because *I* was afraid he was going to clam up and avoid me because of what I'd said.

So I beat him to the punch.

I left before he could hurt me.

I didn't give him a chance, because I couldn't even give myself the chance to be vulnerable for once in my life.

I'd *really* fucked up.

"No," I said, my shoulders sinking.

"When's your next event?" Cade asked.

I looked at my phone, noting the Pride kickoff was our last event.

Tonight, that was my shot.

My chance to make things right.

To set the record straight.

Once and for all.

CHAPTER TWENTY-EIGHT

Penn

"ALL RIGHT, I think that's everything," Archie said as we loaded the empty boxes into the dumpster out back behind the firehouse.

The annual Jasper Springs Pride Show was always one of our biggest events. Most of the businesses took part in it, each with a table that boasted their wares or business brochures.

The firehouse always sold their calendars, the pet hospital usually had animals that were up for adoption out to meet, and all the restaurants and food services usually donated food or sold snacks.

I'd always loved the event, because I loved making the cookies and desserts in bright colors, something different than our usual bear claws and croissants or wedding cakes.

Although this year, I felt like it was an entirely new experience.

I surveyed the crowd, searching for Mitchell. I knew he would be here as we'd discussed all my events ahead of time, and both had agreed this event would be the last, and the biggest, and since the Show usually happened the Friday before the Pride Parade, Mitchell had promised to have something ready for the social media page that we could use.

But that wasn't why I was looking for him.

I needed to tell him the truth.

I wanted to be with him, and while I knew the road of a relationship would be full of uncertainty, I knew that was what I wanted because I loved him, and that was enough for me.

I only hoped it would be enough for him.

"I'm going to grab some grub from the taco truck. You want anything?" Archie asked as I adjusted the plate of cookies at the bakery table.

"No, I'm good," I said.

Archie nodded. "Your mom said she and your dad would be here around four to relieve us."

I nodded. I was nervous, still unsure of how my dad would take the news his son had turned a new gay leaf, but I supposed there were harder things to deal with.

Like saying out loud, "I love you, and I want to be your boyfriend."

Archie sped off, leaving me to man the ship myself.

I still hadn't seen Mitchell, but that didn't mean he wasn't there. Being the most popular photographer in town, I was sure he was snapping more than just my cakes and cookies today.

"Hey, Penn!" Amy's voice broke my train of thought, and I tensed immediately.

I turned to see her, standing there in a bright pink mini dress, her gold curls bouncing against her shoulders. She looked like the epitome of Elle Woods in

Legally Blonde.

She smiled brightly, standing next to a woman who was adorned in a white tank top, jean jacket with an array of pins, and a rainbow belt.

The woman's dark hair was braided with glitter, her green eyes standing out against all the bright colors. She was beautiful.

"Amy..." I said, feeling my blood freeze.

"Fancy meeting you here," she said.

I shrugged. "My family's bakery works this every year," I said, hoping to dodge any invitations.

"That's cool. I've never been. This is my first Pride, like, in general since..."

I watched as her cheeks blushed, and her friend smiled softly.

The world slowed to a standstill.

"Oh, Jesus, I totally spaced, uh... Molly, this is Penn. My ex-boyfriend," she said the words sweetly, almost endearingly.

Molly smiled, nodding as she looked me up and down. "I see," she said.

I never felt so judged in all my life. Seriously.

"Hi," I said awkwardly.

Amy giggled. "Penn, this is Molly. My girlfriend."

Girlfriend.

The bubble popped as understanding dawned on me.

Amy reached down, grabbing her *girlfriend*'s hand, smiling from ear to ear.

"You're..."

"Bi," she said with a smile. "Though, I'm still kind of new to the whole... *dating* girls part."

"Huh," I said, at a loss for words, blinking furiously.

"That's why I wanted to talk..." she said softly. "I know we weren't, like, end game or anything, but I didn't want you to hear it from someone else. I—"

My shoulders loosened as her words hit me.

"I know we had our ups and downs, but I always felt like we were good friends, you know?"

I did know. Throughout our relationship, talking to Amy was one of the easier parts. The sex wasn't bad, but it wasn't great either, and felt like it was just part of what we were *supposed* to do.

Which made a lot of sense as I looked

at her *ease* with her girlfriend. I never made her smile like that.

The sight made me think about Mitchell.

"How did you know?" I asked.

Amy blinked. "Know what? That I was bi?"

I shook my head. "No. How did you know it was going to work out... with... your girlfriend?"

Molly shrugged, her green eyes lit up with amusement. "Because I'm a total catch, obviously."

Amy rolled her eyes, shoving her playfully. "And humble, too."

I watched as Amy smiled, flipping some hair over her shoulder. "Honestly, the thought of being without her was worse than the thought of what could have been."

I smiled genuinely. I understood her words one hundred percent.

The thought of being without Mitchell made my entire body tense.

Wondering what we could be if I was open to a *real relationship*. The possibilities made me want to try.

Maybe I could be happy, too, like Amy and Molly.

I didn't want to live a lie anymore. I wanted to be genuine, and that started with my feelings.

That started with Mitchell.

The rest of it, I'd figure out.

"I'm happy for you. Both of you," I said, grabbing a tray of sugar cookie rainbows, offering it to them.

"Thanks, Penn," Amy said, and she bit into the cookie, her eyes rolling back with satisfaction. Molly and I both laughed.

"It was really nice meeting you," Molly said as she pulled her girlfriend along.

"We should totally get together sometime!" Amy said through a mouthful of cookie as I waved at her.

"Absolutely," I said with a smile, just as Archie came back with a container full of tacos.

"Who was that?" he asked.

"My ex-girlfriend," I said, with a smirk. "Who apparently likes pussy way more than I do."

Archie laughed, popping open his container. "Mitchell's over at the Jasper Springs Pet Hospital table hanging out with his friends."

Archie's words settled on me.

He was here.

Just across the road.

"Go," Archie said, waving me off. "Go get your man and all that," he said, biting into his taco, crunching away.

I didn't have to be told twice.

CHAPTER TWENTY-NINE

Mitch

I CLICKED AWAY on my camera while Cade and Weston handed some kittens over to a group of girls.

"You're stalling," Dawson said, nudging me in the shoulder.

"Don't you have to go wash a fire truck or something?" I nipped, watching the look on Cade's face as he placed the kitten in the arms of a woman with vibrant blue hair.

"Today is your lucky day. I'm off duty."

"You're about to need a medic if you

don't get off my ass," I quipped.

"All I'm saying is, this is your last event together, right? You got here early. And you haven't left Cade's side since you arrived. I know he's your emotional support animal and shit, but come on, Mitch."

I lowered my camera, turning to glare at Dawson, who had the audacity to look perturbed.

At me!

Didn't he know he was the resident pain in the ass?

"I'm just—"

"You say it's complicated, I will punch you," Dawson grumbled.

"I'm working!"

Dawson hummed annoyingly. "Mhm. Well, here he comes, so buck up, Buttercup."

"What?" I asked, turning to see Penn walking across the street, right toward us, his hands stuffed in his jean pockets.

His bright blue polo shirt stood out against his pale skin, blond hair blowing in the wind. I half expected to hear some Bananarama playing behind me, or for someone to offer him a bottle of shampoo.

Fuck, he was so pretty.

My gaze caught his, and the smile that spread across his face was enough to melt an iceberg.

Instinctively, I snapped a photo.

"Hey," he said as he approached my lens.

I slowly lowered it, my heart catching in my throat. Behind me, I could hear Dawson humming away annoyingly.

"Hey," I replied, at a loss for words.

Up close, he smelled like sugar and cinnamon, like whipped vanilla frosting.

Like a fucking cream puff, making my mouth water.

I noticed the tiny rainbow flag pinned on his shirt, and couldn't help but smile.

"I, uh, can we talk? Somewhere?" he asked, running a hand through his golden locks.

Cade nodded at me from my side, clearly telling me I should leave.

But a part of me was certain this was it.

The inevitable crash and burn where Penn was going to tell me he didn't feel the same way.

That he just wanted to be *friends*, or

worse.

Friends who sucked each other's cocks.

Which wouldn't have been a bad arrangement, if I didn't want more.

And with Penn, I'd always want more.

I'd want to wake up in bed with him curled around me. I'd want to have impromptu dinners in his kitchen, and cupcake frosting fights, and drunken karaoke make outs.

I'd always want him in a way I could never have him, if we were just *friends who fucked around.*

"Yeah, sure," I said, gripping my camera strap. I followed him across the street to one of the park benches in the small park, which was crawling with overflow traffic from the show.

Couples and groups of friends were littered all across the lawn, and it sort of reminded me of our date.

Where we'd watched a bunch of cover bands and made out under the fireworks on the lawn.

"What, uh, what's up?" I said, trying to sound nonchalant. Stoic.

I knew what was coming, and there was no avoiding it.

"I, uh, I've been thinking about... stuff," Penn stammered, biting his bottom lip.

I sighed.

"About... us, I mean," he said the words softly, and it was like a knife to my heart.

Here it comes.

"What are we?" he asked the words curiously. "Because I saw you at that wedding, and we were strangers. Then, we talked online, and you were someone I hired, and then we hung out, and you were my friend, and then we went on a date and you were...." His voice trailed off, and he closed his eyes. "You weren't a friend, anymore, but I wasn't sure what you were. What you are, to me."

"I get it, Penn. You don't have to... Fuck, we don't have to do this. I just..."

"No, I need to do this. I need you to hear this," he said firmly, and I sighed deeply, my palms sweaty against my strap.

"I know I don't always know what I'm doing. Hell, I'll be the first to tell you I have no realm of experience here. I've never felt for anyone what I feel for you."

I looked into his glassy blue eyes and

saw the fear there.

The unknown.

Instantly, my panic melted, my nerves fraying at the edges.

I reached out to wipe a tear from his face, shoving my own fear aside as curiosity got the best of me.

"What do you feel, Penn?" I dared to hope he felt the same.

That somehow, some way, I hadn't lost him.

"I—" he stammered, biting his lip. "I think I'm totally in love with you, Mitch."

My heart leaped at his words. I blinked, wondering if I'd imagined them. If I'd lost my marbles completely and gone full on insane.

"Penn..."

Penn slid his hand over mine, chewing his lip once more.

"I know I'm not the best boyfriend, period. I don't always know the right thing to say, or the right thing to do. But I know when I'm with you... I *want* to be the best boyfriend."

He licked his lips, his glassy eyes sparkling with truth as my heart swelled with pride, with joy.

"I want to be *your* boyfriend," he said

the words, and they pierced my heart, lighting me up with the brightest, fullest feeling in the word.

Love.

"Yes," I murmured, pulling him toward me, claiming his lips with my own. "Fuck, yes," I whispered, and he kissed me. I could feel his lips turning up in the corner with a smile as his hand settled on my hip, his tongue sliding into my mouth.

I kissed him back deeply, with all the love I could. When we broke apart, we both breathed heavy sighs, his palms hot against my thigh.

"So... that's a yes?" he asked sweetly, flashing his bright eyes up at me.

"Yes, Penn. I want to be your boyfriend, too." My heart soared.

CHAPTER THIRTY

Penn

MY HEART BEAT so loudly in my chest, I wondered if Mitchell could hear it.

I wiped some stray confetti from my shoulder as he opened the door to his apartment. We'd been here before, only days ago, but somehow it felt like a lifetime.

After my parents had shown up to take over for the remainder of the event, I was excited to just be a part of the event.

With my boyfriend.

Well, and his friends, of course. We

even ran into Amy and Molly again, and then Mitchell asked if I wanted to come over to his place and actually watch a movie and just hang out.

I settled against him, appreciating the warmth of his arm around me and I couldn't stop smiling.

I stared at the half-empty box of pizza on the table as Ace Ventura did his best parrot impression. I didn't get the movie, but watching Mitchell laugh his ass off, was enjoyment enough.

"What?" he asked, glancing down at me. "Do I have pizza on my face?"

My heart beat away in my chest as I turned my head and took in the sight of him.

"I just... a lot has happened since we were here last," I said.

Mitchell leaned in, giving me a sweet, quick kiss, and I melted once more, kissing him back.

"One of these days, we're going to make it through an entire movie," he whispered, his grin making his eyes light up with mischief.

I slid my fingers against the hair at the nape of his neck, slipping my tongue into his mouth with a confidence I hadn't possessed the last time I'd been here.

I slid my hands down his frame, wiggling them underneath the hem of his shirt.

Mitchell laughed against my kiss.

"Today is not that day," I whispered against his lips as I ran my hand over his abs, up over his solid chest.

Mitchell cursed, sighing deeply as he pulled his shirt off.

"There's always tomorrow," he said, shaking his head, running his hand through his hair.

I leaned forward, kissing him once more, letting my hands explore his bare chest, fingertips running over his nipples.

My cock throbbed in my pants, and I wondered how I'd ever lived without this.

Without *him.*

As if he could read my mind, he tugged at my shirt, and I let him remove it.

We both sat there, on his couch, shirtless, visibly aroused, and exposed in a way that had nothing to do with skin.

Mitchell stood up, holding his hand

out to me.

I didn't think twice about taking it.

He pulled me close, into an embrace that was as tender as it was strong, melting my heart. His lips moved slowly against mine as he breathed deep. His hand settled on the flesh of my hip, warm and solid.

"I love you," he said. "I thought today, at the show, when you asked to talk, I thought..."

I searched his gaze, noting the glimmer of fear.

I knew it well, because up until recently, I'd also been afraid.

But as I stood there, shirtless, in *my boyfriend's* living room, I knew there was finally nothing to be afraid of.

Not when we were together.

"I know," I whispered, my heart in my throat. I leaned in, capturing his lips with mine once more. I settled one hand on his waistband, the other on his neck. His pulse thrummed beneath my palm, beating in time with my heart.

"I wanted to tell you I loved you, yesterday, but you ran off."

Mitchell gently pulled away from me, walking toward the hall. He stopped, his shoulders dropping as he breathed, "I ran off because I thought I'd scare you away."

He turned to me, his dark gaze glistening with promise.

With a vulnerability that hadn't existed yesterday.

I took slow steps toward him, my cock twitching with need. I didn't feel embarrassed about grabbing myself, and I didn't feel embarrassed about the way his gaze fell to my hand, or the way he looked at me.

Like I was truly *his*.

I stopped in front of him, reaching out to brace myself against the wall with one hand, picking up his hand with the other.

I let out a deep breath as I placed it over my heart. His palm was warm against my chest and I liked how it felt there.

Mitchell smirked as I said, "I'm not scared of what I feel when I'm with you."

His gaze softened as I leaned in closer, bringing our bodies together. His fingers slid over my pec, taking my nipple in between his thumb and forefinger as he pinched and pulled, causing my cock to twitch, and me to stifle a moan.

"Not anymore," I said, moving my hands to gingerly unbutton his jeans, unzip his zipper.

Mitchell shook his head as he let out a dark chuckle. "Is this what you want, Cream Puff?" he taunted, sliding his hand down over my stomach, to cup my cock through my jeans. "You want to be the prince charming?"

His thumb rubbed my cockhead through my jeans, and I pushed his pants down to the floor. I gazed at him up and down, taking in the sight of his nakedness in its entirety. Amidst the dark shadows and the amber light, he was by far the hottest thing I'd ever laid eyes on.

And he was *mine.*

The truth coupled with my desire was a heady cocktail, and I thought about all the times he'd been patient with me and my insecurities.

A world of possibilities and unclaimed moments lay ahead of us, and I, for one, was more than excited to venture into the unknown with him.

I took a step back, watching as he

stood there patiently waiting.

Waiting for *me* to call the shots, to tell him what to do, I realized.

I slowly unbuttoned my own jeans, divesting what was left of my clothes. Mitchell's heated gaze fixed on me, trailing over me with lust and love.

So much love, it was like a sugar high.

I grabbed my cock, sliding my hand along my shaft as I gazed at him.

Mitchell praised me constantly, and I couldn't deny I liked it, how his words made me feel.

So, I took a page out of his book as I closed the distance between us, catching his gaze as I let go of my cock, bracing my hands on the wall, pinning him beneath me. His gaze glistened with excitement as I pressed myself and my leaking cock against him.

"You are, without a doubt, the hottest thing I've ever seen," I said, finding my voice.

"Oh yeah? Is that so?" he drawled, grabbing *both* our cocks together in his hand.

Instinctively, I thrust myself against him, but it was no use, I needed more.

Mitchell moved his hand slowly up and down as he jacked us both, and I captured his lips with mine.

A thousand thoughts ran through my brain, a thousand wants, a thousand *needs*.

The foremost being one I never thought I'd dream in a million years, but that felt more right than anything else.

Tuned into me like he was, he only whispered, "Tell me what you want, Cream Puff."

I let my hand drop along his body, pulling him away from the wall. I slid my fingers over the supple flesh of his ass, my heart in my throat as my fingertips slid over his seam.

Mitchell groaned from the touch, which only fed my desire more.

"I want you," I said, letting my fingernails dig into the skin of his cheeks. The lust in my voice was foreign, but somehow it felt so undeniably true I couldn't refute it.

The need to be inside of him, possessing him, was both scary and exhilarating because I'd never *wanted* anyone as badly as I wanted Mitchell.

"How do you want me, baby?"

Mitchell teased, using his thumb to spread our combined wetness along my shaft.

I swallowed harshly as the words fell out of my mouth. My heart thumped in my chest as I held his gaze, like a blazing fire.

"I want to fuck you."

Mitchell smiled the sexiest grin I thought I'd ever seen, his dark hair falling in his eyes as he leaned up to nibble my lip.

"Is that so?" he purred, pushing me gently as he dipped toward the shadows. I followed him like a moth to a flame.

Toward his bedroom.

Bedroom.

A part of me felt scared as he turned on the light, keeping it low enough to see, but not bright enough to be distracting. I watched as he sauntered toward his bed, the dark black and gold geometric comforter standing out against the black, padded headboard.

There was something exhilarating about standing in his bedroom, feasting my eyes on his amber-lit flesh. My cock throbbed as the air kissed my moist skin, and I had to wrap my hand around my cock to quiet the need for touch.

Mitchell gazed at me over his shoulder as he opened his bedside table drawer.

I took one step closer, watching his shoulders knit as the sound of a cap popping echoed in the space. Then I took another step, then another, until I was in front of him.

I braced my fingers on his shoulder, letting them travel over his skin and I wrapped my arms around him, pulling his body flush against me.

Mitchell turned in my arms, and I leaned forward, kissing him with all that I was.

And what I was, was a ball of nerves, of sensation, of fear and love, and excitement and uncertainty.

But underneath his touch, underneath his kiss, I was safe.

I could just be... me.

"Yes," I breathed against his lips, stepping forward, nudging his legs apart with my knee.

Mitchell fell back against the bed with ease, and I tumbled with him. He shifted us both back, wrapping his leg around my hip, our cocks brushing together, hard and wet.

I couldn't help the moan that escaped my lips. A cool wetness kissed the edge of my cock, familiar but also foreign.

One glance to his nightstand, and I noticed the open bottle of lube, which was like a splash of cold water to my system.

I wanted this, wanted him.

But it had also been a while since I'd had sex—let alone anal—with anyone.

And I'd certainly never done it with a *guy*.

My nerves threatened to upend me, but Mitchell only slid his fingers through my hair, pulling my lips to his.

"You're in charge here, Penn. If you want to stop..."

I shook my head, crushing my lips to his, his words giving me the strength they always did.

Letting me know it was okay to not be okay.

That it was okay to be nervous.

I slid my hand over his thigh as I ground myself against the cool wetness of his puckered opening, his cock sliding against my stomach, leaving wet trails of precum along my skin.

And when I looked in his eyes, seeing the desire, the love there, I forgot all about my nerves.

I kissed him softly, letting my tongue caress his, and I slowly tilted his hips up with one hand, gripping myself with the other, lining myself up. My breath hitched as the head of my cock pressed against his slick, lubricated entrance, and the rest of the world around me blurred.

For a moment, we lay there, intertwined, panting against one another as I inched my way inside his heat, breaching the tight ring of muscle. Mitchell's cock was solid and wet against my abs, throbbing as I kissed him. I grabbed his hardness in my hands as instinct took over, and my cock throbbed in the tight space and I started to move.

Mitchell rocked his hips in unison with my thrusts as I built a rhythm, slow and steady.

His insides clenched me tightly, driving me absolutely mad.

I didn't want to stop.

Not now, not ever.

"Fucking hell, Penn..." Mitchell grunted, wrapping his other leg around my hip, pulling me deeper, until I'd completely bottomed out.

"Mitch..." I grunted, my words starting to disappear, my linguistics systems taking a siesta again.

Words were hard to form when I felt *this* good.

His cock throbbed in my hand as I brushed my fingertip over his slit, wet and sticky precum coating both my hand and his shaft as I quickened my pace. There was nothing but the sounds of our breath, of wet skin slapping together, of guttural grunts and whispered curses as the flames consumed us both.

CHAPTER THIRTY-ONE

Mitch

I WASN'T PARTIAL to topping or bottoming, but underneath Penn, I became someone else entirely.

I became the one who was needy, desperate for release.

I became the one begging for mercy as he caressed my cock while filling me to the brim.

Penn slid his thumb over my weeping cock, his lips hot against my neck as he breathed against my ear. "Tell me what you want, Cupcake."

I wish I could have laughed at his

choice of endearment, but the way he spoke, his voice deep with desire and command, I would have answered to fucking Princess.

I'd held Penn beneath me plenty of times now, and I'd coaxed him, guided him to tell me explicitly what it was he desired, both because I needed to hear it, but also because I liked hearing him *beg*.

Now the tables had turned, and I was desperate for *his touch*.

"I want you to make me come, baby," I breathed as I bit his lower lip. His cock throbbed inside of me, spurring me to grind my aching, wet cock against him once more.

"Please," I added, just to be a smartass.

Penn quickened his thrusts, nailing my prostate over and over, and it didn't take long for either of us, really. The minute my blinding orgasm came, I felt a sudden rush of warmth, followed by Penn practically collapsing on me, his breath labored as he squeezed my cock tighter while I came.

I didn't know how long we lay there, connected. Penn curled against me, buried to the hilt as I softened against him. Our legs intertwined together, him wrapped in my arms.

I kissed his temple as he sighed contentedly. "I love you," I said with a smile.

Penn buried his face in my hair as we both rolled over onto our sides, the motion causing him to slip out, as well as his release.

Penn looked up at me with bright eyes full of wonder and hope.

And when he told me he loved me, I knew I'd finally found the person who made me whole.

CHAPTER THIRTY-TWO

Mitch

I OPENED PENN'S passenger door, my camera bag slung over my shoulder.

While he slept, I stayed up to work on photos, mostly because I couldn't sleep after being so wound up over what had happened.

We'd fucked.

Well, technically, I was the one who'd given it up, and I was okay with that. If that was what my little Cream Puff wanted, I'd gladly let him fuck me six ways from Sunday.

Because, to be honest, Penn made a

pretty good top.

Who would have thought the shy, quiet, boy next door baker would be so fucking *hot* in the bedroom?

It's always the quiet ones.

Penn climbed out of the car, grinning like a kid on Christmas.

It was after ten, and I had to admit it was weird to see someone else open the shop.

"Hey, Penn!" Archie called out, waving at us both. "Mitchell..."

"I hope you had fun time last night," Penn's mother said, flashing a smile as she pulled her son in for a hug. I headed for the office, stopping in my tracks when she said, "I meant you, too, Mitchell."

I turned to see Penn blushing as his mom held him close.

"I have a feeling we'll be seeing a lot more of one another," she said.

I looked from Penn to his mother, raising an eyebrow at Penn, who looked like he wanted to disappear completely.

That was the moment his dad came out of the office.

"Mitchell, so nice to see you. I hope you have those photos from the show ready. I really want to start getting some posts circulating this week. It's a big week you know."

"Uh huh. Actually, I, uh, have the files right here. Stayed up almost all night finishing them."

Penn broke away from his mother as he came to my side.

"You didn't have to—"

"I wanted to," I said, flashing him with a smile. I caught his father's judgmental gaze as he looked from his son to me, half expecting him to yell, or cuss me out, or something.

But he only vacated his chair, looming in the doorway as he said, "There better be some actual pictures of baked goods and not just candids of my son."

Frozen, I attempted to speak as his mother hit her husband in the stomach.

"Leave the boy alone, you're embarrassing him," she chastised, flashing me a smile.

Penn turned an adorable shade of pink as his father narrowed his eyes, moving to let me into the office.

Penn entered first, as I stood in the alcove, staring up at his father. As I brushed past him, he whispered to me.

"Break his heart, I'll break your bones. Got it?"

I looked up at him, the obvious love and the genuine acceptance making me feel as if I could perish right there on the bakery room floor.

"Yes, sir," I said, entering the office, setting my gaze on the most perfect man in all of Jasper Springs.

If Penn and I could survive our own selves, surely we could survive anything else the world threw at us.

Including overprotective fathers.

I sat in the office chair, hooking up my external drive, and bringing up the photos as his father left the office, replaced by an excited Archie.

"All right, Mitchell, let's get this show on the road," Archie said, slapping his hands together.

One by one, I cycled through the photos. Cakes, cookies, prep work, well-lit signs, customers.

I was always proud of my work, but these were certainly stand outs in my portfolio. From the smoothness of the buttercream, to the employees, I was more than proud of the shots I'd captured.

Because the bakery wasn't just a business to Penn or his parents, or even Archie.

They were a family, a community, a place to relax, and indulge.

"These are phenomenal, Mitch," Penn said in awe.

His mother smiled. "I agree. Do you do prints? I might want to order some of those portraits of my pride an joy you took," she said sweetly.

Penn blushed, and I couldn't help but smile.

"I think that can definitely be arranged," I said.

Archie smirked. "Maybe I'll grab some for my profile," he said, preening like the pain in the ass he was.

But nothing could sour my mood, not even Archie.

And when Penn smiled, rolling his eyes, too, I knew this was only the beginning.

EPILOGUE

Three months later...
Penn

"OKAY, THIS TIME you're actually singing solo," Archie touted at me over his beer.

I rolled my eyes as I leaned on the high top, sipping my Angry Orchard. "I believe it's your turn to embarrass yourself on stage this evening," I bit back.

"Cream Puff's right. You managed to fly under the radar last time, but tonight is your penance," Mitchell drawled as Cade made his way down from the stage.

I checked my phone once more, waiting for Amy's text. I'd finally taken her up on her invitation to hang out, which wasn't terrible. In fact, once we both actually started talking, it was more cathartic than anything. I even told her about Mitchell, and she suggested we all hang out.

So, I invited her to our monthly karaoke hang out with Mitchell's friends.

"She'll be here, don't worry," Mitchell said, nudging my arm.

I glanced at him, feeling instantly at ease. No matter what was bothering me, Mitchell always seemed to have a way to soothe my nerves.

"All right, next up we have... Archie? Is there an Archie in the house?" Will, the DJ, called out.

I smiled smugly as I watched Archie's jaw tense.

"You..." he hissed out.

"Your audience awaits," I teased, taking another sip of my drink, just as a familiar voice pulled me from my victory.

"Hey, Penn!" Amy sing-songed, sliding between Mitchell and I for a hug.

And when I hugged her back, it didn't feel awkward or unwelcome.

Amy smiled as I gave a quick hug to Molly, too.

"Amy these are my... friends, Cade, Weston, Dawson, and Nolan. Guys this is... my... friend, Amy, and her girlfriend, Molly."

A resounding hello and polite introductions were made as Henry came to our table, dropping off our drink refills. On his heels was none other than Grayson, his boyfriend, and...

I turned to see the newlyweds with their bridal party in tow, sidling up to a high top two spots over.

Archie belted out the worst rendition of Mariah Carey's *Heartbreaker* I'd ever heard, while Giselle all but skipped over to our table.

"Hey!" she said with excitement, hugging Mitchell. He kindly returned the favor as she leaned back, setting her hand on her newly formed bump.

Archie finished his set as Mitchell and Giselle dived into a discussion about baby photos as Drew Axel took the stage with his boyfriend, Taylor.

"How long is Drew in town?" I asked, cutting into their discussion.

"Wait, you know him?" Amy pressed.

I shook my head. "I don't *know* him, know him. But I've met him like once. He has a house here, I think."

Grayson nodded, sliding his arm around Henry. "He does. Comes and goes though, guess that's the life of a rockstar."

Drew and Taylor's rendition of Taylor Swift's *Love Story* was a much better performance than Archie's screeching.

I think Dawson was actually better than him, and that was saying something.

"Giselle!" Aaron called from across the way, waving her over to the table where her bridesmaids slash friends, Julie and Mia were sitting, as well as a man who looked very familiar, but I couldn't place.

Though he kind of looked like the guy in the porn I watched all those months ago.

But I'm sure that was just my mind playing tricks on me.

"You karaoke?" Dawson asked, nodding at Amy.

"Who me?" she asked, looking around confused.

Dawson nodded.

"Oh, uh, I mean, not usually..."

I caught Molly's gaze, and we shared a knowing look. Amy was a natural carpool karaoke fan.

As Drew and Taylor wrapped up their star performance, I couldn't help but think about just how much my life had changed in the course of three months.

I'd come home from college lost. Single, alone, and wishing that I could find someone to love, someone to share my passions with.

And as I sat in M's Place, surrounded by drinks and laughter, I felt like I'd finally found everything I was looking for.

I found the man of my dreams, but I'd also found a family.

A place where I finally fit in.

I raised my glass, looking at Mitchell.

"To new friends, and new beginnings," I said with a smile, as the beginning of a classic Freddie Mercury song sounded across the stage.

"To new friends and new beginnings," Mitchell said, clinking his glass with my bottle, and one by one everyone chimed in.

"I'll drink to that," Dawson said.

"Me too," Cade said as he raised his glass.

And when we all brought our drinks back down, I shot my boyfriend a glance.

"So you want to catch a movie after this?" I smirked.

Mitchell picked up my cue without missing a beat.

"That depends. Are we going to actually watch the movie, or are you just trying to get in my pants?"

"That depends on your choice of movie, Cupcake."

Mitchell sipped his drink, his dark gaze full of mischief as he shrugged.

"One day, Cream Puff."

I settled my hand on his hip, casting him a devilish smirk of my own. "Today is not that day," I said as I pressed my lips to his.

Mitchell melted into my kiss as the sounds of Amy crooning out Whitney Houston's *Higher Love* sounded in the space around us.

"There's always tomorrow," I whispered against his lips.

Mitchell gripped my hips as he kissed me.

And as we made out in the middle of

M's Place, surrounded by laughter and drinks, and friends, and love, I looked forward to what tomorrow would bring.

Thank you for reading Mitch and Penn's story. If you enjoyed this book, please leave a review. Even a few words means so much to me.

Thank you!

~*Evie Riley*

OTHER BOOKS BY EVIE

Federal Protection Agency
Mason
Rafe
Ryzen
Cooper
Noah
Damien
Sebastian
Gabe
Logan

Ruthless Empire
Courting Danger
Chasing Danger
Kissing Danger

Smokejumpers
Hawke
Cyrus
Jase
Gage
Jackson
Xavier

EVIE RILEY

Jasper Springs
Cade
Dawson
Drew
Grayson
Riley
Mitch

From The Edge
Shattered
Runaway
Jaded
Rescue
Hidden
Tormented

Gray Vale Pack
His Fated Mate
His Wounded Warrior
His Healing Heart

ABOUT THE AUTHOR

Evie Riley is a prolific, neurodivergent author known for her captivating MM romance novels. She has gained a significant following and topped the LGBT+ action and adventure bestseller charts with her series.

Evie's writing style often explores dark and gritty themes where her men must overcome difficult obstacles in their search for love, but she has also ventured into sweeter small-town romances, incorporating tropes like enemies-to-lovers, friends-to-lovers, age-gap, and forced proximity. She is known for crafting engaging romantic suspense novels and has a knack for creating interconnected series worlds that keep readers invested.

EVIE RILEY

Interestingly, Ms. Riley has hinted at exploring new genres, such as Alien Omegaverse Romance, in the future.

Outside of writing, she enjoys spending time at the beach and has a quirky personality, described by her partner as ranging from cute to deadly, depending on her blood-chocolate levels.

Evie spends her nights writing bad boys in love, and her days wrangling the sweet boys she loves.

www.ingramcontent.com/pod-product-compliance
Lightning Source LLC
Chambersburg PA
CBHW071415200726
48294CB00002B/399